The Bold House Murders

The Bold House Murders

EUGENE FRANKLIN

STEIN AND DAY/*Publishers*/New York

First published in 1973
Copyright © 1973 by Eugene Franklin
Library of Congress Catalog Card No. 72-96294
Published simultaneously in Canada by Saunders of Toronto, Ltd.
Printed in the United States of America
Stein and Day/*Publishers*/7 East 48 Street, New York, N.Y. 10017
ISBN O-8128-1567-X

ACKNOWLEDGMENTS

I want to particularly thank Lieutenant Colonel Allan D. Bell, Jr., and Mr. Charles R. McQuiston of Dektor Counterintelligence and Security, Inc., for the hours they spent explaining and demonstrating the fascinating capabilities of the Dektor psychological stress evaluator.

E.F.

1

"If I were you, I'd eschew the mushrooms."

Eschew? The speaker was Bentinck Bold, one of the people we were checking. Tall, slender, with a neatly trimmed golden beard and mustache framing his bony face, he was smiling at me with a lot of white, irregular teeth.

"Why?"

"They're fantastically unappetizing. Unless you have the palate of a goat."

"No one cares for my Mushrooms Ossie-Tabasco," said Osborne Kilgore, "and I picked them this morning with my own genius fingers. The fingers that rattle the typewriter and entertain millions." He paused and then said, "And pour millions into Bold House."

"Hear, hear," said Bentinck Bold.

"Won't anyone join me in Mushrooms Ossie-Tabasco?"

There were no volunteers. Those nearest the large outdoor oven and charcoal broiler made polite excuses. "Thanks, no, Ossie, not today." One said, "The last time I ate your mushrooms, my stomach turned its face to the wall and rejected me for two weeks."

Kilgore's big mouth turned down in a mock grimace. "Then you'll have to be content with filet mignon." He spooned up a large helping of mushrooms onto his own plate.

Osborne Kilgore. Worth ten million dollars dead, and probably several times that figure if he lived out his normal span. Thirty-seven years old, and one of the biggest "big money" novelists of the decade, he managed to grind out a best seller every year. Even in an era of low-budget film-making, each of his books somehow became a super-colossal motion picture earning astronomical box-office millions. Balding, short, and wide-shouldered, he looked more like one of the men who might have stumbled in to move your furniture. Except that the furniture jockey would't have worn Kilgore's glasses. They were campy, oversize, and super-round. The thin gold temple bars rested on ears that stood straight out in almost perfect half triangles.

His being worth ten million dollars dead was the reason for our being there. Wickersham of England was betting ten million that Kilgore stayed alive. Seemingly it was a good bet. Kilgore was reasonably young, in buoyant good health, and had no dangerous hobbies such as sky-diving or auto racing. The policy made sense, too. Five million for his widow, Kathryn Kilgore, for estate liquidity, and five million for Bold House, his publishers, in a sort of "key executive" policy. Don't ask me to explain estate liquidity or the habits of the very rich. I'm a former freak who dropped out of college after two years of being unable to relate to practically any learning. But it seems that when you have a big estate and most of your money is tied up in property and other noncash investments, you need insurance cash for estate liquidity so that inheritance taxes won't force your heirs to sell out everything at a loss. Or something.

Dale Jones, the vice-president we deal with at Wickersham, had no qualms about the policy. At first. Then the Sabatini case broke. The young Texas oil millionaire who was insured for fifteen million, then got shot to death in less than a year? It had developed that he was a millionaire in reverse. He *owed* about ten million dollars. And had a few unsavory connections too.

Nasty suspicions were raised in insurance circles. Executives of some companies ran around wildly looking for smoke and shouting at each other to evacuate the premises. The Wickersham people were only faintly apprehensive when they took a second look at the Kilgore policy. The premium was a sweet one hundred and eighty-five thousand dollars a year, and that helped. Furthermore, Osborne Kilgore was a highly legitimate multimillionaire. His associates and beneficiaries were legitimate and respectable. Reasonably respectable. To make sure, however, they called in Berkeley Barnes, my boss. In addition to being one of New York's top private investigators, Barnes is a lawyer and can tell you everything you've always wanted to know about estate liquidity.

"Frankly, I don't know what to tell you to look for," Dale Jones had said. "Just nose around the situation and see if you come up with anything irregular." If disaster struck, he wanted it on the record that he had taken reasonable precautions.

Kilgore had an estate on the shore about a hundred and sixty miles northeast of New York City, a penthouse in Manhattan, a villa on Ibiza, a townhouse in London, and an apartment in Paris. At the moment he was in the second easiest place for us to get to, his shore place at Swigatchit. We made it in about two and a half hours in Barnes's Porsche, including a stop for gas. And these middle-aged guys like Barnes think pot is dangerous!

With charcoal broiled filets mignon of the nine-dollar-a-pound variety, it hardly seemed proper to describe Kilgore's party as a cookout. But that's what it was, a champagne-and-caviar cookout, with plenty of help around to do the heavy work. Kilgore had invited us when Barnes called him for an appointment. While it was not mentioned, Kilgore knew about the Sabatini case and was amused that staid and British Wickersham might be panicky. So we were spending a beautiful spring day mixing business with nine-dollar steaks and champagne, a happy combination. I was the only one paying much attention to business, however.

If they ever give an Oscar for hypochondria, Barnes will have gold statuettes all over his Sutton Place apartment in a few years. He's the world's biggest psycho-sick. At the moment he had found a soul mate, an attractive middle-aged woman with a lot of long, thin steel needles sticking out of one shoulder. At first I thought it was some kind of mod extravagance of dress. Then it occurred to me that she was certainly an acupuncturee, and it was frightening to think that Barnes might expect me to take it up to cure his chronic sinus condition. *Twist that fifth needle a little to the right, will you, Larry?* I don't mind carrying around Bufferin, Pepto-Bismol, codeine, Donnatal, tranquilizers, placebos, and other assorted emergency medications, but if I'm going to be forced into surgery, I need more training.

"Sure you won't try my Mushrooms Ossie-Tabasco?" asked Kilgore, eyeing my already overloaded plate.

"No, I'm chicken," I said.

"Because I picked them? Man, I've picked wild mushrooms for years without a single fatality. I'm an expert."

"Thanks, I'll pass them up." If this guy was running around eating wild mushrooms, maybe Wickersham did have something to worry about. At least it would be an item to report, which was probably more than Barnes would have to contribute, unless they were interested in the latest in Chinese needlepoint.

I wasn't sure about exactly what we were supposed to investigate, other than to take a close look at the beneficiaries and possibly the financial condition of Bold House. The Texas millionaire who had been murdered had been in serious financial difficulties. Instead of being worth the sixty million dollars his estate was reputed to total, he owed ten, part of it to loan sharks with organized-crime connections.

The beneficiaries were all present at this Wedgwood and Tiffany silver cookout, providing an opportunity for a cursory look at least. Bentinck Bold, president and part owner of Bold House, a small but successful and highly regarded publishing company; his sister, Christiana Bold-Jepson, also part owner of Bold House; and Kathryn Kilgore, wife of Osborne, would share the ten million. Indirect beneficiaries would be the Reverend Robert Bold-Jepson, husband of Christiana, and Barbara Bold, wife of Bentinck.

The Reverend Bold-Jepson was beautiful. His mod-length hair was a helmet of shining, burnished copper brushed down to within an inch of his eyebrows. Deep blue eyes, large and widely spaced, stared with feverish intensity. He had regular, almost feminine features and the flawless, milky complexion of the rare redhead who doesn't freckle. Put his face on a different body and you'd have a gorgeous woman. His voice, however, was deep and professionally trained.

"Are you one of Kilgore's flunkies, or one of Bentinck's flunkies?" he asked me, wafting a strong one-hundred-proof breeze in my direction.

"I'm one of the insurance flunkies."

"Oh."

"Wickersham of England." When you're doing insurance work, you seldom identify yourself as a private detective. Soils their image.

"Oh yes. I've heard about Ossie's big ego-trip policy." He sighed, blowing some more hundred-proof my way. "I understand the premiums are close to two hundred thousand. Enough to feed a village of starving Peruvians for two years."

I nodded and moved away, settling down with my plate at one of the small tables dotting the terrace. He followed me, pulling out the chair opposite. "Hope I didn't offend you? There are so many ass-kissers here, I assumed you were one of them." He twisted backward to grab a passing waiter. "Bring me a Haig Pinch. And bring this man something to go with his steak. Burgundy. Bring him Burgundy."

This cat was some reverend. I might take up going to church.

He turned back to stare at me with electric intensity. I could feel the waves bouncing off my forehead. "I did offend you. I'm sorry."

"No you didn't."

"I'm sure I did."

"Not at all." I carved a bite-size piece of filet mignon, which required very little effort. I've cut tougher cheesecake.

The waiter returned with two bottles and assorted glasses. Pinch bottle Haig and Haig, and Burgundy. Bold-Jepson examined the label on the Burgundy. "Nineteen sixty-four. Good year." He handed it back to the waiter to open, then reached for the Scotch, pouring himself a satisfying dollop.

Osborne Kilgore swaggered over, pausing at our table to

glare at Bold-Jepson. "You were skinny-dipping with Kathryn last night."

Bold-Jepson raised one eyebrow. "Is that bad?"

Kilgore leaned on the table, brushing my elbow. "If you want to go skinny-dipping in my pool, at night, alone, you'd better goddamn well skinny-dip with your own wife."

The waiter shoved the ritual sip into my hand. I smelled and sipped and nodded, a little nervously, and handed him the glass to fill.

"Don't be childish, Ossie," said Bold-Jepson. "Kathryn and I, well, it was like taking a bath with my sister."

Osborne leaned further over the table. "I know I should laugh at that one. Ha." He waggled a stubby forefinger at Bold-Jepson. "You know what you are? You're a lousy exhibitionist. In twenty years you'll be one of those guys who wears a raincoat and no pants and flashes it, scaring old ladies."

Bold-Jepson bared some perfect teeth. "Go away, Ossie, before I lose my temper."

"You're a lousy exhibitionist. I'm better hung than any man in this whole goddamned crowd, and when I skinny-dip, I skinny-dip *alone*, in the ocean."

Bold-Jepson stood up. "Ossie, take off those glasses."

Bentinck Bold hurried over. "What's going on here?"

The reverend glanced at him. "This pornography maven is trying to make something over the fact that Kathryn and I went swimming together last night."

"Skinny-dipping!" yelled Kilgore.

Here I was enjoying the best steak I have ever eaten in my whole life, and drinking some of the best vintage wine I've ever tasted, and these two creeps had to start a row, practically in my plate. I moved a few inches away from Kilgore and sliced off another piece of filet mignon.

"Ossie, everybody skinny-dips. What's the matter with you?" asked Bentinck.

"In a crowd," Kilgore yelled, "not a twosome, alone, at night, in my pool!"

"Oh for Christ's sake," said Bentinck.

"Did you hear what he called me? The pornography maven! This *phony* called *me* the pornography maven!"

Bold-Jepson's lip curled. "Maybe *maven* was a bit strong. If you ever wrote about honest sex, I guess you'd have to experience it first." He leaned on the table, projecting his face in Kilgore's direction. "Kilgore, you're a titillator of frustrated women. Your books are without any redeeming social values. With a little work, and attention to male prurient needs, you can be *king* of the pornographers."

Kilgore took off his glasses and threw them on the table, almost in my plate. I moved a few more inches away and sliced off more filet mignon. If Kilgore started swinging, I would move to another table, taking my plate and the bottle of wine with me. This was Bentinck Bold's problem.

Kilgore bent over the table and jutted his chin in Bold-Jepson's direction. "*NewsScope* called me the *great* storyteller of the decade. The new Somerset Maugham."

Bold-Jepson rolled his blue eyes upward. "*NewsScope*'s book reviewer was a truly great Kennel Club editor before they shifted him. It was a tragic loss to the dog world."

I grabbed my plate and the bottle. To heck with the glass.

Kilgore cocked his fist, but Bentinck gripped his arm before he could swing. "Come on, Ossie, he's just needling you. Don't let him push you into making an ass of yourself."

Kilgore jerked his arm loose and yelled at Bold-Jepson, "You lousy parasite, you *live* off the money *my* books make for Bold House! If they're pornography, you don't even have pimp status. You're just a latrine orderly in the whorehouse!"

Bentinck draped his arm around Kilgore's shoulders. "Come on Ossie, cool it. Don't let him needle you. You're too *big* to let him get to you this way." He tried to steer Kilgore away from the table.

Bold-Jepson picked up Kilgore's glasses and said, "Don't forget your teenybopper specs, Somerset."

Kilgore snatched them.

"And get one thing straight, Great Storyteller, I've never touched a penny of Chris's income, and don't intend to. We don't *need* money that badly."

Kilgore settled his glasses on carefully. "Good. It's just possible you may not have so much of it around in the future." He pulled away from Bentinck, and the two walked away, Kilgore leading.

I went back to my filet mignon with relief. It was getting cold.

Bold-Jepson eased back into his chair and picked up his glass. "I really should stay away from these parties. There's something about Osborne Kilgore that brings out the worst in me."

"His novels?"

Bold-Jepson smiled. "His novels are fairly lively trash. It's probably his lack of humility that bugs me. He thinks they're great art."

I poured some more of the really terrific wine, for which I could thank Bold-Jepson. "Are you English? I mean, the hyphenated name?"

"No. I'm a victim of women's lib. Chris said, 'If I'm going to take on your name, you've got to take on mine.'" He poured himself some more Pinch. "In a way I suppose it makes sense. Sometimes I feel a little silly being known as Bold-Jepson. My father, bless him, thinks it's downright communistic. But then our whole life-style is a mystery to Appleton, Wisconsin."

"Is that where you're from?"

He nodded. "Chris tends to be unrealistic. Carry this hypenation thing past one generation and you have our daughter, for instance, becoming Daphne Bold-Jepson-Hillary-Swartz."

"You don't have a daughter named Daphne?"

"Of course not. We have no children. But should we have one named Daphne, suppose she had one named, say, Janet. When Janet married, she might become known as Janet Bold-Jepson-Hillary-Swartz-Bluestein-Johnson-Fenelli-Smith.

In five generations we would be reduced to addressing each other as 'Hey, you.' "

I poured some more Burgundy. "This is really great wine. I'd like to visit your church someday."

He stared at me, his friendly smile fading, replaced by the electrical intensity I had felt earlier. I could sense the radar waves rippling past my ears.

"Our church is not for everyone. I don't mean that in an exclusive or snobbish sense. Our appeal, intellectually, is to those ahead of their time. To those who seek spiritual heights far above the levels of awareness that they may find, say, in the more popular and more circumscribed religions."

I finished off the filet mignon. Absolutely fantastic to the last bite.

"I'd still like to visit. Who knows, I might be up to it, intellectually, I mean." While it was part of my job to get to know the beneficiaries, I was genuinely interested in seeing the Reverend Bold-Jepson in the pulpit.

He fumbled in his jacket pocket, smiling again, and brought out a card. "Why not? You'll be welcome," he said, handing me the card.

I glanced at it and put it in my pocket. "Robert Bold-Jepson, Ph.D., Minister, Church of the Expanding Awareness." The address was in the Village, in New York.

"Thanks. I'll look forward to it."

"What is your position with the, ah, insurance company?"

"We investigate unusual situations. Keep an eye on exceptionally big risks."

He nodded. "I see." He thought for a few seconds, then said, "I see. If Ossie developed a passion for skin-diving in shark-infested waters, you'd be grievously perturbed."

"We would, yes. In fact, Wickersham might grieve themselves right into canceling the policy."

He laughed. "I would say you have little to worry about. Ossie is a cautious man."

I looked up to find Christiana Bold-Jepson hovering over us. A slender, fragile-looking young woman with short, wind-blown boyish hair, thin eyebrows slightly arched, big eyes, and a large but attractive mouth.

"Ossie is difficult enough. Why do you have to put him down every time you see him? He's in a rage."

I stood up.

"Chris, this is—uh, I'm afraid I—"

"Larry Howe. From Wickersham of England."

"The insurance company for Ossie's big policy," said Bold-Jepson.

Christiana gave me a careful look. "How do you do. I've met your associate, Berkeley Barnes. A delightful man."

"Boss, not associate."

She smiled and turned back to Bold-Jepson. "Really, Bob, *why*—"

"He started it. He was publicly castigating me. Accusing me of skinny-dipping and fornicating with Kathryn."

"Were you?"

"Skinny-dipping, yes."

Her face developed some hostile lines. "Why did you find it necessary to skinny-dip with Kathryn? Alone, at night, in *his* pool?" Christiana had already been briefed.

"Because she was there. If you remember, I told you I was going for a swim, and asked you if you wanted to come along."

"I don't remember that."

"You were lying there reading a book."

"I was asleep when you left."

"You were not."

"I was. I woke up later and wondered where you were."

"You put the book down and said, 'Good God, no.' "

"That was three nights ago, not last night. What do you see in that chubby cream-puff kitten anyway?"

"Nothing, love."

"Who's a chubby cream-puff kitten?" Unnoticed, Kathryn Kilgore had wandered up, and was now standing about five feet away.

"You are, dear," said Chris.

16

I wouldn't have called her chubby. She was nicely rounded. In fact, her figure was her best asset. Her long, straight black hair was okay too. Her face I didn't care for, perhaps because she was angry, and her tight little mouth gave her a mean look.

Kathryn moved closer, looking slyly malicious. "When Bob asked me to meet him for a late swim, I had no idea that we were going to create a scandal. The whole thing's ridiculous."

"Bob asked you to meet him?"

"I did not."

"Bob!" Kathryn looked at him sorrowfully.

With an irritated toss of her head, Chris turned and walked away. Kathryn and Bold-Jepson stared at each other, exchanging some meaningful sighs.

Barnes came strolling up with an elderly Chinese. Dr. Wu Tsi had thick-lensed glasses and a slender neck one size too small for his collar.

"Dr. Wu," Kathryn asked, "can acupuncture cure allergies?"

Dr. Wu smiled. "Cure is a very large word. Let us say, it can relieve the physical distress of allergies." He shrugged. "How permanent? Sometimes yes, sometimes no."

"Mrs. Bold-Jepson is allergic to chubby kittens."

"Ah. Very interesting." He peered at her carefully. "But must they be chubby?"

"She's teasing you," said Barnes.

"Ah. She pull my leg." He laughed politely.

Kathryn glanced at Bold-Jepson, her eyes warm and possessive. "Do you think I'm a chubby kitten?"

Bold-Jepson shook his head. "Tigress."

2

"There's something ugly about this situation, but I can't quite put my finger on it," said Barnes. We were headed back to New York.

"Slow down, or we'll sustain injuries that even acupuncture can't cure."

He eased down to eighty-five. "Massive egos in conflict."

"Who?"

"Bentinck Bold, Kilgore, Christiana, and the reverend. Undercurrents of tension and hate. I could feel them. A miasma of bitter vapors."

"You didn't mention Kathryn Kilgore. She's causing some bitter vapors too."

"How?"

"She's got a thing going with Bold-Jepson, and doesn't seem to care who knows it."

He glanced at me and we almost crawled up the back of a Volkswagen poking along at seventy. Before I could yell, he swerved around it with a quick glance in the rear-vision mirror.

"Sticky," he said.

If he was referring to the palms of my hands, he was right.

We rode in silence for a while, Barnes demonstrating how he could win the Indianapolis 500, down-gearing to ninety on the curves.

"We'll give it a week or two. Check every angle we can think of. I've got bad vibes about the whole thing," he said.

In Manhattan traffic, we always do plenty of straining against our seat belts. Barnes alternates between wild spurts and standing on his great grabby brakes. He dropped me off at my two-room pad in the East Seventies which costs me two hundred and eighty a month, which is a lousy ripoff, but what can you do?

I called Isabel and suggested that she come over and bring a pizza. She suggested that *I* come over, and that *I* bring the pizza, which is pure female chauvinism. I don't mind buying the pizza, but I hate to go to Isabel's because her roommate, Kathy, turns me off. Way off.

Isabel has very long, straight, clean-looking straw-colored hair, and a life-style that alternates between being a concerned citizen and a flippant copout. When she's concerned, close the hatches and hide. It's Bella Abzug for president, and Shirley Chisholm for director of the F.B.I. On the copout side, we have a joint savings account. For a year or two on some little island in the Aegean. She's beautiful and aggravating, and we'll probably go and get twin tattoos someday, which is as good as getting married.

"Here's the pizza, and here's a bottle of wine, and please tell me Kathy isn't home so I can enjoy the pizza," I said.

"Kathy wouldn't eat any of your precious pizza, even if she were home." Isabel gets defensive about Kathy.

"It's not that. It's the bad vibes. They curdle the mozzarella."

"It's your think tank that's curdled. What am I saying, tank. I meant thimble."

I poured us each a glass of wine and pulled two pizza slices apart. "Don't bug me. I've had a hard day consorting with the rich and famous, not to mention about five hours of nerve-wracking driving with Barnes."

"I thought Barnes was a good driver."

"He is. But he shouldn't drive the way he does. He's too old. Your reaction time is slowed down when you get old."

"He doesn't look old."

"He must be at least forty."

There were thumping and scrambling noises at the door, the metallic scratch of a key jabbing unsuccessfully at the lock.

"Go away! Leave me alone, you *pig*!"

The door popped open. Kathy stumbled in and immediately tried to push it shut. Her pushing met resistance on the other side.

"Don't push me out, dingbat!"

"Go away! I never want to see you again! You're a slimy pig fink!"

I took a bite of pizza, sorrowfully. Couldn't a man eat a meal *anywhere* in peace in this world?

The door received a mighty shove and her current boy friend lurched into the room. His beard covered everything but his eyes and a red nose, and he had the best Afro hairball I have ever seen on a nonblack.

"Look, dingbat, I said I was *sorry*. I'm not leaving until you look at this thing in a mature way."

I gave Isabel an 'I told you so' look. "Would you two shut up and let people eat a civilized meal?"

Kathy glared at me, then turned back to scream at him, "Guess what, Kathy, I don't have any money. That's the last time you guess-what me, you smelly gorilla!"

Rednose waved his arms around like a guy trying to hail two cabs. "Listen, fishface, you always have at least ten bucks in your purse. How was I to know—"

"Well, I didn't!" she yelled.

"I've paid plenty of times."

"I've never been so drably humiliated in my life!" She turned to Isabel. "This *rat idiot* asks me to have dinner with him. I should have known better. For once I forgot, you have to carry money with you when *he* invites you to dinner."

He strolled over and helped himself to a slice of pizza. "You're just sore because that stupid manager made a scene."

"It was *my* watch we had to leave!" she yelled.

He gobbled down some of the pizza. "I offered him my belt. I paid twenty-five dollars for this belt."

Kathy rushed into the bedroom and slammed the door. He started to follow. Isabel stood up and pointed dramatically to the hall door. "Michael. Go."

He paused, shrugged and started out. "Tell her to grow up. The whole thing was just an unfortunate occurrence. I personally will redeem her watch when I get paid next week."

I have a recurring nightmare. When Isabel and I find our sun-drenched little island, Kathy will be there ahead of us.

If Barnes didn't pay me three hundred a week, I would deeply resent his calling me on a Sunday morning. That's pretty good bread for an ex-guitar player with no talents for corporate upward mobility. Like the undertaker's assistant, I recognize that we sometimes have to work Sundays.

"Osborne Kilgore is dead!" he yelled into the phone.

I held it a couple of inches from my ear. "Well, criminy, I didn't kill him."

"I'll pick you up in fifteen minutes," he said, and hung up.

Osborne Kilgore was dead? There would be some frenzied hand-wringing at Wickersham of England. Ten million bucks. Bad show, old boy. Very bad show. We'll all smart for this one!

I was down on the sidewalk waiting when he pulled up. Dale Jones eased up right behind, driving a battleship-gray Rover.

"Would you like me to ride up with Mr. Jones? Sort of keep him company?"

"No."

"I could show him the way."

"He knows the way."

I climbed in with a sigh. Fasten seat belts and no smoking please until we're airborne. Maybe it was just as well. I hate to see a man cry, and Jones had looked like he was going to do just that.

"What happened to Kilgore?"

"Drowned. I have a miserable damned headache."

I found the right plastic container, uncapped it, and handed him a couple of Bufferin. He chewed them up without water the way he does, the thought of which always gives me a touch of pucker power.

"Was he drowned in his pool, or the ocean?"

"Ocean. Why?"

"He mentioned that he went skinny-dipping in the ocean alone, at night. This was due to modesty."

"Modesty?"

"He was modest about how well-proportioned he was. Didn't want to make other men jealous."

"You're kidding."

I looked back. Dale Jones's Rover was nowhere in sight. Probably couldn't drive very fast, with his eyes tearing up.

"Anyway, it sounds like an accident."

"Hmmm."

"There's a suicide clause that lets Wickersham off the hook, isn't there?" I had done my homework and read the famous policy, fine print and all.

"Very hard to prove, in a drowning. Unless he left a note."

"You'd better slow down. I think you've lost Jones."

He glanced in his rear-vision mirror and slowed down a trifle. "I can't see Kilgore committing suicide. Unless possibly he discovered he had a fatal illness."

He lit one of the ten filter-tip cigarettes he allows himself per day, manipulating the steering wheel with one elbow. Then, switching elbows, made a note in the small notebook he carries to enter the number and time of each cigarette consumed. I gripped my wrist to keep my left hand from reaching over and grabbing the wheel.

After one hand was back on the wheel I relaxed. "Ten million bucks. That could put a lot of companies out of business."

"Ten million wouldn't put Wickersham out of business. They have assets of over two billion. Anyway, part of the loss would have been reinsured."

I looked back. The Rover was again in sight. But why mention it?

"It's still a very nasty blow."

He puffed away gratefully. "An understatement. I've never seen Jones so shook."

Bathed in warm spring sunlight, the vast old seaside mansion looked too friendly to be the scene of tragedy. A State Police cruiser was parked in the driveway, but the place seemed strangely inactive and quiet.

The maid was obviously distraught and walked away, leaving us standing in the hall. Kathryn Kilgore appeared shortly, weepy, but by no means in a state of collapse.

"I suppose it hasn't really got to me yet," she said, "I just can't seem to accept it."

"Sorry to intrude," said Barnes, "But—"

"I understand." She nodded to Dale Jones, and gave me a brief look of recognition. "I suppose you'd better come in the library."

She led us down the wide hall to a large, book-lined room with floor-to-ceiling glass facing the sea. There were only two occupants. An elderly man was seated at what was probably Kilgore's desk, and a short, broad-shouldered man standing, staring out at the surf. He turned as we entered and looked us over carefully.

She introduced us. At least Barnes and Jones; I had to supply my name to Sergeant Marino of the State Police. The elderly man was Dr. Frisbie, the Pell County coroner. He had been scribbling on a pad. He finished quickly and threw the pen down.

"Just writing the little lady a prescription. Help her sleep tonight. Terrible thing." Looking closely at him, he appeared to be at least eighty. His voice had a high quaver.

"What is your, uh, interest in this, uh, situation?" Marino asked Barnes. Jones was still in a state of shock, and I guess Barnes looked the most intelligent of our group.

"We represent Wickersham Insurance Company. The deceased was insured with us. For ten million dollars."

Sergeant Marino's broad face registered wide-eyed disbelief. He ran one hand through the fringe of curly black hair circling his bald spot, then thumped his forehead with the palm of his hand. "Ten million *dollars*! You must be kidding. Nobody's insured for ten million dollars."

"I wish we were, old boy," said Jones, coming alive.

Kathryn walked to the door, then turned, her hands clasped before her. "I guess you can get what information you need from Sergeant Marino and Dr. Frisbie. So, if you'll excuse me—"

"Perhaps we can talk to you later?" asked Barnes.

"If you wish." She left, leaving the door open.

"Ten million dollars," said Marino, soft awe in his voice. "You fellows have my sympathy."

Jones fished out his black briar and started filling it, giving Marino a stiff nod.

The details were simple enough. Kilgore had gone for a late-night swim, which he did frequently. This Marino couldn't understand, because the water was still cold enough to freeze the ass off an Eskimo. But it seemed to be well established that the occasional dip was Kilgore's custom. A brief swim battling the icy water made him sleep better. He was known to be an excellent swimmer. The surf had washed him up onto the beach, and his body had been discovered by Christiana Bold-Jepson. Awaking early, she had decided to take a walk before breakfast. None of the other guests had been awake. Kathryn had slept through the night without missing him.

"You'll perform an autopsy, of course," said Barnes.

"Why?" asked Dr. Frisbie. "As clear-cut a case of drowning as I've ever seen."

"Nevertheless—"

"I've been a doctor for more than fifty years. Hell, there was sea water in the guy's lungs. Enough to gush out when I turned him over and applied pressure."

"Still, we'll have to insist upon an autopsy. He was a good swimmer. Why does he suddenly drown?"

Dr. Frisbie stood up impatiently. "It was the cold water

that done it. Hell, anybody can get a sudden cramp in water that cold."

Jones waved his pipe in Frisbie's direction. "See here, old boy, with this amount of money involved, we must insist—"

"*I'm* the one who says whether there'll be an autopsy in Pell County."

Sergeant Marino lit a cigarette, staring at Frisbie. "I think they should have their autopsy, Doctor. Ten million bucks isn't exactly change. I can see possible repercussions later if—"

"Then goddammit they'll pay for it."

"The state will pay for it."

"We'll gladly pay," said Barnes. "In fact, I'd like to bring in our own pathologist. A top man."

Jones cocked an eyebrow at him. Weren't they losing enough money, without paying a big fee to a pathologist? He started to speak, but changed his mind. Probably decided it was better to leave no stone unturned.

Sergeant Marino turned to Barnes. "As a matter of policy, it works this way. Your pathologist can be present, observe and suggest. He can even assist, I guess, if our pathologist agrees."

Barnes nodded. "I'm only concerned that the autopsy go further then finding salt water in the lungs and then packing it up."

Marino found an ashtray and stubbed out his cigarette. "I understand. You want all the organs examined. In case someone slipped him a mickey before he went for his swim."

"I'm not implying that, necessarily."

"It's better not to leave any loose ends."

"Exactly," said Jones.

Dr. Frisbie shrugged. He strolled to the door. "Well, then, I'll leave it in your hands, Sergeant. Sheer waste of money, but, as you say—" He gestured disdainfully and walked out, almost bumping into Barbara Bold, Bentinck's wife.

Of all the women at yesterday's cookout, Barbara Bold was by far the most attractive. Long taffy-colored hair parted in the middle framed her face. She had widely spaced gray eyes, a high forehead, a slightly turned up nose, and a mouth just irregular enough to be intriguing.

She nodded to Barnes and Jones, smiled at me, then spoke to Marino.

"Kathryn has no close relatives, and I, well, I've volunteered to handle the arrangements. I've spoken to the mortician and he would like to know—"

Marino nodded. "I'm afraid you'll have to wait a day or so. Until the autopsy is completed."

"Autopsy?"

"The insurance company has requested one. The circumstances being what they are, I also feel this is necessary."

Barbara bent her head slightly and her hair almost covered one eye. "Circumstances? I don't understand. Dr. Frisbie said he was quite plainly"—she hesitated—"quite plainly drowned.

Marino said, "With ten million dollars involved, we have to make certain he was drowned accidentally."

She stared at him, widening her eyes. "How else could he possibly have drowned?"

Marino smiled apologetically. "It's just a matter of touching all the bases, Mrs. Bold."

"I see." She straightened her head, brushing her hair to one side. "Then I suppose we shall have to wait. Unless Kathryn wants to fight it." She paused for a few seconds. "Suppose she does?"

Marino's smile twisted downward. "That's her privilege. But I'll tell you right now, she'll lose. After some nasty publicity."

Dale Jones had stoked up his briar and was puffing furiously. He removed it from tightly clenched teeth and said, "We shall not pay one penny of the claim unless a complete and thorough autopsy is performed."

Barbara turned to him. "Heavens, I didn't realize you felt that strongly about it."

"We do."

"The arrangements are rather complex, and take some planning, that's all."

Barnes said, "What are they, if I may ask?"

She glanced at him. "After the funeral service, it was his wish to be cremated, and for his ashes to be deposited exactly on the North Pole."

"Jesus Christ," Marino said, hardly audible.

"That will certainly take a little doing," said Jones.

"I said it was complicated. Not only that, Dr. Bold-Jepson's schedule is rather tight. We've got to know when the funeral can be held so he can work it in."

"The Reverend Bold-Jepson is going to perform the funeral service?" asked Barnes. He glanced at me. I had told him about the nasty quarrel.

"Yes."

"This was Osborne Kilgore's wish?"

"No. It's Kathryn's wish."

3

After Barnes had talked to Dr. Harvey Schoenfield, a well-known authority on forensic medicine, and had arranged for Dr. Schoenfield to be present at the autopsy Monday afternoon, he called a motel in Swigatchit to reserve rooms for us. It was during this call that Bentinck Bold strolled into the library. Catching the gist of the conversation, he said loudly to Barnes, "No need to book rooms."

"Hold on," said Barnes into the phone. "What?"

"Hang up. Plenty of space here."

"I'll call back," said Barnes, replacing the handset.

"This place has thirty-five rooms. I insist that you stay here."

Barnes smiled. "It would seem that it should be Mrs. Kilgore who insists."

Bentinck shook his head. "Take it that Barb and I are acting for her. The poor girl is near collapse."

Barnes glanced at Dale Jones. Jones nodded. It would be handier being on the scene. "All right," he said, "if you're sure we won't be imposing."

"No imposition. This place is run like a hotel. Plenty of help, and a constant stream of visitors coming and going. Ossie liked company." He eased his lanky figure into one of the leather armchairs. "Williams, the butler, will take care of you." Bentinck took a slim gold cigarette case from his jacket pocket, opened it, and stared at the cigarettes thoughtfully.

"Now I wonder where I'll find a pilot willing to fly over the North Pole low enough to, ah, deposit the ashes exactly?"

Eyeing Bentinck's cigarettes hungrily, Barnes said, "You do have a problem." He consulted his little cigarette notebook and shook his head sadly. "I suppose losing Kilgore will be quite a blow to Bold House."

Bentinck lit a cigarette and replaced the case. "Yes, of course. We'll miss Ossie." He sighed. "However, Bold House did very well before Ossie came along, and I suspect we'll make out well enough without him."

"Especially with five million dollars' consolation," said Barnes.

Bentinck gave him a quick look. "Ah yes, there's that."

"I'm curious," said Barnes. "Why would a publishing house need such a large sum as a hedge against the possibility of losing a star author? Suppose, for instance, he had simply decided to change publishers? Presumably it wouldn't bankrupt you?"

Bentinck stood up and stretched. "It's rather complicated, but Ossie drove a rather hard bargain. We were protected somewhat by a series of three-book contracts, but we had to guarantee tremendous expenditures for advertising, publicity, and sales promotion. If we had lost him between, say, book one and book two of a three-book series, we would have been in quite a hole financially."

"A five-million-dollar hole?"

Bentinck laughed. "Not that much, of course. Ossie had rather grandiose ideas. It was his wish to be insured for ten million, and quite typically he expected us to pick up half the fantastic annual premium."

"Not to mention the expense of placing his remains on the North Pole," said Barnes.

"That will be Kathryn's expense."

I suspected that if Kathryn had her way she would just mail Kilgore's ashes in a plain brown envelope marked *To Santa Claus, North Pole.*

Barnes strolled over to an end table next to one of the sofas and picked up a small photograph of Kilgore. It was a scaled-down print of a Karsh portrait which had been on the cover of *Time* magazine. He studied it, then walked over and handed it to Bentinck. "Would you say this reflects the real Osborne Kilgore?"

Bentinck stared at it and Barnes watched Bentinck closely.

"No, not really. Karsh somehow manages to get some drama and interest into any face. Ossie was essentially a petty, narrow man, and a thorough bore."

He handed the photograph back to Barnes. "Even his writing was a bore."

Barnes raised his eyebrows.

"Without Hal Zimmerman's editing, he wouldn't have even been publishable. He was prolific, and he researched his material thoroughly. When he finished a book, he would turn in a manuscript of over a thousand pages. Then it would be poor Hal's job to chop and rewrite, cut out the clichés and the old movies, and shape up the puerile dialogue. When Hal finished, there would be four hundred pages and a readable novel."

Barnes was mildly astonished. "I see. I'm surprised an editor would be willing to put in that much work."

"Ordinarily I expect they wouldn't, unless they were working with someone of the stature of Thomas Wolfe. At least, not on a writer's first novel. Of course, after Ossie's first book was such a commercial success, Hal was more or less trapped."

Jones, who had been quietly puffing his pipe and staring out at the water, said, "You know, it has just occurred to me that there is no earthly reason for me to be here until the autopsy results are in. I think I'll head back to New York."

Barnes agreed. Jones wasn't contributing much to the scene but a heavy pall of depression anyway. There were handshakings all around, and Barnes accompanied him out to his Rover.

Bentinck collapsed into another of the big armchairs.

"How did you get into this type of work, Larry?"

I was surprised that he remembered my name. "Why, sort of drifted into it, I guess."

"I imagine you get involved in some interesting situations."

"Sometimes. Yes."

"Have you ever uncovered any large insurance frauds?"

"Barnes has."

He nodded. "I'd like to hear about them someday."

Barnes returned before I had to reply. He stood, looking undecided, then walked over and picked up the photograph of Kilgore again. "Do you think Mrs. Kilgore would mind if I borrowed this for a day or so? I'll take good care of it."

Puzzled, Bentinck said, "Help yourself. There are dozens of them around. Ossie was not known for his modesty." He scratched his golden beard thoughtfully. "But I can't imagine what you would want it for. Certainly there's no question of identity? We all saw him before they, ah, took him away."

Barnes opened the back of the frame and slipped the photograph out, then placed the picture carefully in his inside jacket pocket. "I'm not concerned about identification. Just call it a whim."

At lunch I was surprised to find four other houseguests still present. The big house was so quiet I had visualized a mass exit following the discovery of Kilgore's body early in the morning.

The dining room was huge, and the large polished mahogany table, shaped in a giant oval, could seat at least forty. Our small group congregated at one end. It consisted of Bentinck and his wife Barbara, Hal Zimmerman, editor-in-chief of Bold House, with his wife Deborah, Upton Eads, Kilgore's agent, and his wife Susan, and Barnes and myself. Kathryn was having a tray in her suite.

Over turtle soup liberally enhanced with good sherry, Bentinck said, *"De mortuis nil nisi bonum.* But I can't help thinking, Hal, that it must be a relief to you to contemplate a future without another Osborne Kilgore novel to edit."

"Amen," said Zimmerman. In spite of his high forehead and shiny-bald egg-shaped pate, Zimmerman had a youthful, dramatic look about him. Straight, bushy eyebrows on top of alert, deep-set eyes, a large but straight nose, a heavy brown mustache and full chin whiskers, gave him a somewhat long-faced, saturnine appearance.

"*De omnibus rebus et quibusdam aliis,*" he said.

I whispered to Barnes, "I got the 'de mortuis' bit, but what's *that*?"

"Prolix," Barnes muttered, "he's saying that Kilgore was verbose."

Upton Eads put his soup spoon down with a loud clink. "You people kill me. You're sitting here enjoying a dead man's hospitality and making snide remarks about him. In Latin." Square faced, with baggy eyes and a stern mouth, Eads looked more like an aging police sergeant than a literary agent.

"Who says we're enjoying it?" asked Bentinck. "We're here because Kathryn asked us to stay and help out."

Eads's mouth curled. "Yeah. The grieving widow." He picked up his spoon. "You know what I think? I think you're all damned glad to see poor old Ossie shuffle off, so you can collect ten million bucks."

Susan, Eads's wife, began to cry. A sultry brunette, she was at least twenty-five years younger than Eads. He reached for her hand. "I'm sorry dear, I—"

She jerked her hand away, stumbled to her feet and hurried from the room. Glancing around at the others belligerently, Eads continued to eat his soup.

"Now you all quit being nasty," said Deborah Zimmerman. "We're all under a strain." She had a broad Southern accent, a mass of curls on top of a pixie-bright face. "We're all going to miss old Ossie."

"I'll miss him about the way I'd miss a boil on the end of my nose," said Zimmerman.

"Hal!" said Deborah.

Eads stood up and threw his napkin on the table. "I think I'll have lunch somewhere else," he said, and stomped out, heavy-footed.

"His golden goose just died," said Zimmerman. "We should show respect."

Bentinck examined the bottle of sherry idly, as though wondering whether to add some to his soup. "Somehow I cannot be sentimental about Osborne Kilgore's passing. Over the years he became a monumental pain in the rear. Mammon tied us to his chariot. We'll be picking the splinters out for a long time."

"Did Chris go into town?" asked Barbara Bold.

"Of course. This is Sunday, remember?" said Bentinck.

"The Reverend Bob's big day," said Zimmerman.

"And Chris's day to hover, with claws extended while his female parishioners crowd around and gurgle," said Deborah.

"He's a beautiful man," said Barbara.

"Ah ha," said Bentinck. "Don't let me catch you skinny-dipping with him at night, alone, in *anybody's* pool."

Barbara smiled and touched his arm. "Don't worry. I prefer your rugged, manly ugliness."

"Thank you. I'll accept the first two, reserve decision on the third. Some of our authoresses tell me I'm beautiful." He turned to Barnes, as though suddenly remembering that we were being neglected. "We probably seem callous to you."

Barnes smiled. "At least you're not hypocritical."

Bentinck cocked his head slightly. "Actually it has been a terribly shocking experience."

"It certainly has," said Zimmerman, "and however much I had grown to dislike Ossie, I would not wish death on him."

Barbara Bold put her fork down and looked thoughtful. "I question Kathryn's taste," she said.

"What?" asked Bentinck.

"Insisting on Bob for the funeral service."

After lunch Barnes and I drove into Swigatchit to stock up with shaving gear, toothpaste, Pepto-Bismol, and other necessities. I had a feeling it was going to be a big Pepto-Bismol week, because Barnes takes his client's problems very seriously. He suffers when their fortunes dip. Ten million dollars was some dip, and the situation looked relatively hopeless.

"It's too bad we're involved," he said on our way back.

"Wickersham certainly can't blame you."

"My name will be associated with it, all the way up the line. When anyone asks who handled that Kilgore disaster, the answer will be 'Berkeley Barnes.' It doesn't help."

I said "Hmmm" and concentrated on his driving. Someone has to.

After depositing our purchases in our respective guest rooms, we wandered downstairs and outside to inspect the grounds.

Kathryn was sunning herself on a plastic chaise longue near the swimming pool. As was proper for her widowhood, she was wearing a conservative black bikini.

Barnes pulled up one of the tubular aluminum chairs and sat down. I took off my jacket, folded it over the back of another chair, and followed suit.

"You must be uncomfortable in those clothes," said Kathryn. "There are swimming trunks in the cabana, if you want to get some sun."

"I might take you up on that, later," said Barnes.

She pouted. "I think it was mean of you to insist on an autopsy. It makes the whole tragedy sort of sordid."

Barnes stared at her with his *kindly* look. "Under the circumstances, it would seem to be necessary."

"I couldn't care less about the insurance, personally. I've always felt it was bad luck."

"Bad luck?"

"Bad luck to bet that heavily against fate."

"Oh."

"The money means nothing to me. There's already more than I'll ever need."

"Aren't there any other relatives?" Barnes asked.

"A brother in Scotland. They couldn't stand the sight of each other. I cabled, but I doubt that he'll come."

Barnes consulted his cigarette notebook, decided he was entitled. Reaching for his cigarettes, he said, "I understand the Reverend Bold-Jepson is going to conduct the funeral."

Kathryn gave me a quick look, remembering no doubt that I had been a witness to their meaningful sighs. "Funerals are for the living," she said. "Ossie is beyond caring. It will be a much more beautiful and memorable thing for me if Bob handles it. After all, I *am* a member of his church."

"The Church of the Expanding Awareness?" I asked.

"Yes."

"He invited me to visit it."

She turned her head to look at me sleepily, her eyelids drooping. "Each person can rise as far as he or she wills it. Others are chained to mediocrity."

I had a feeling my chains were jingling. "Is there a service in the evening, on Sunday?"

She lifted one knee provocatively, displaying her beautiful legs to better advantage. "The church is open until midnight on Sundays. Bob works very hard."

I had been mentally searching for an excuse to get back to New York and Isabel. Like Dale Jones, I had begun to feel that nothing much could be accomplished before we learned the autopsy results. We couldn't cross-examine anyone intensively without more information. If Barnes wanted to sit around and mope, okay. I preferred to mope with Isabel.

Kathryn lifted herself to her feet gracefully. She trotted to the diving board, bounced a few times, then cut through the air in a beautiful swan dive.

"I've just been thinking," I said to Barnes. "It might be useful if I went back to New York and attended services at the Church of the Expanding Awareness. See what kind of setup the Reverend has. After all, Sunday comes but once a week."

Barnes finished his cigarette sadly and crushed it out. "Why not?" he asked. "You can take the Porsche." He dug in his pocket for the keys and handed them to me. "And take it easy. You're not all that expert when it comes to driving at high speeds."

I let that pass.

"As long as you're going to be in New York, stop by my place and ask Mitsui to pack my bag with fresh clothes."

Mitsui was an elderly Japanese who functioned as valet,

cook, butler, and chauffeur when required. Barnes had tried marriage earlier on, unsuccessfully. Mitsui gave him fewer allergies.

On my way to New York, I got a ticket for going sixty-nine miles an hour in a sixty-five-mile-an-hour zone. Which I think is pretty disgusting.

"My boss jets along this turnpike at ninety or a hundred and never gets stopped," I said, "and *I* get a ticket for being four miles an hour over the speed limit."

"Who wants to chase a guy going a hundred?" asked the trooper. "You think I'm some kind of nut?"

In New York, I collected a suitcase for Barnes and a bag for myself, then called Isabel. I had planned to take her to church with me. But after thinking it over, I decided it was not wise to mix her in with business. Certainly not Bold-Jepson business. He was too beautiful. Why expose her to temptation? Suppose she became one of his faithful disciples, throwing Bella Abzug completely overboard? We arranged to meet at nine-thirty.

The Church of the Expanding Awareness was a startling surprise. I had expected something modest. It was housed in a spruced-up old theater which could easily seat a thousand. There were already standees.

Milling around in the huge old lobby were seemingly hundreds of ushers and usherettes, most of them young and beautiful. Purple and gray were the colors. The girls wore purple turtleneck sweaters and gray pleated miniskirts; the men, purple blazers and gray slacks. Most of the men had longish hair, but of the well-brushed, well-groomed variety. As a former freak I could recognize that they were too neat to be acceptable. The type we had called "the plastic people." Mod, but only half with it.

On the stage, a rock group was doing an acceptable job with music from *Jesus Christ Superstar.*

One of the usherettes took my arm, cuddling me a little, and we went for a walk down the aisle, where she found me a seat near the stage. I liked this church.

Music alternated with short announcements by church

officers of various meetings and activities, coupled with pleas for money. They had many activities. Everything from encounter groups to cooking classes. I got the impression that Bold-Jepson's church would be a great place for a lonely person. He or she could spend his or her whole life there.

Eventually I could sense excitement beginning to build. The lights were gradually dimmed and a giant spotlight found one side of the stage.

Bold-Jepson came striding out. He was wearing a brilliant purple cassock with a wide white collar. As the spotlight followed him to the center of the stage, everyone stood up.

He mounted the steps to the low pulpit, raised his arms wide, and said, "Please, good friends, do sit down. Being here with you is honor enough."

They sat down, in waves, as though reluctant to do so. He surveyed the vast auditorium for a few seconds, then began to speak. This was not the ordinary, human-size Bold-Jepson of yesterday's cookout. This was Bold-Jepson Superstar. His voice gripped your attention and held it enthralled. Words flowed out beautifully and precisely in patterns that quickened the emotions. Physically it was as though stimulating charges of alternating current were tickling the heart and mind. Analyzed later, what he had to say was not new. But then, what is?

He said you could be anything you wanted to be, achieve anything you wanted to achieve, by willing it and thinking it hard enough. He said the power of the mind was the most awesome power man possessed. He said that because man was the only creature with a mind complex and subtle enough to make a world of good and evil, it was thus man's responsibility to live for the good. For love, kindness, generosity, sensitivity, honesty. He made you feel big, important, powerful. You held the fate of *good* in your hands. He was a jumbo-size package of charisma.

On my way out, one of the cute usherettes took my arm and led me into an area backstage which was divided into numerous small, curtained cubicles. Ours contained nothing but a small table and two chairs facing each other on opposite sides. On the table were forms, note pads, and a black box that was obviously some kind of electrical gadget.

The girl, who was about twenty and a blonde with a super figure, asked, "Did Dr. Bold-Jepson reach you?"

I nodded. "I dig him. He's really cool."

She smiled. "Then it's time for you to start moving toward the first plateau of awareness."

I glanced at the table. Her big brown eyes were boring holes in me. "Why not?"

"That'll be a twenty-five-dollar contribution."

I must have looked startled. She said quickly, "It's to help make sure you are taking it seriously. The church has to have money to function. But mainly, we want people who are serious about it, people who are willing to sacrifice money as well as time."

I nodded.

"If you're serious about it, you'll be asked to contribute specific sums from time to time. Always within your means, of course."

I reached for my wallet, took a quick peak. I had only twenty-two dollars. "I'm a little short." I grinned. "Don't suppose I could put it on my Everything charge card?"

She reached for my wallet and looked, handing it back to me. "You can, but you'll have to add seven percent."

I almost fell off my chair. This was a real cool church, man. She left me for a minute and returned with the forms and the familiar credit card imprinter. We got the contribution out of the way in a jiffy, and I tucked the receipt away.

"In approaching the first plateau of awareness, you must start on the task of *knowing yourself*."

"That's not easy."

"We're all here to help you. Everyone from Dr. Bold-Jepson down to workers such as myself who are only on the second plateau."

She shuffled through some papers. "The first thing I have to do is fill out a long questionnaire. And it's absolutely essential that you answer the questions honestly, even if they embarrass you. We can't know you, and you can't know yourself, if you lie or rationalize."

"Okay," I said, "go ahead."

During the next half hour I parted with the most detailed, and most intimate, information I have ever been called upon to divulge. Worse than getting a loan for a used-car purchase. My salary, my rent, my debts, my physical condition, my eating habits, my drinking habits, my doping habits (if any), my sex life (good, I told her), my parents (their sex lives too; I could only guess), my employer, my brothers, sisters, uncles, aunts, cousins. My dreams. (Did I ever dream I was having sex with a child? An emphatic *no*.)

Toward the end of the long eight-page form I was beginning to perspire a little, and to wonder whether I owed Wickersham this much invasion of my privacy. What if the questionnaire fell into hostile hands? Worse, what if it fell into Isabel's hands? Or Barnes saw it? Oh well.

My interviewer, whose name was Marianna, sighed as she filled in the last answer. "That just about does it. The rest won't take long."

She opened one side of the black box and pulled out two metal hand grips attached to it by wire. "One in each hand," she said, handing them to me. I grasped them firmly. She flipped a switch and we both watched as the hand moved about three quarters of the way across the dial.

"Wow," she said.

"What does that mean?"

"You're oversexed."

"You're kidding."

She got up, smiling. "Yes, I am. Follow me, please."

She led me to a room fitted out as a small laboratory. "Take off your jacket and roll up your left sleeve."

"Why?"

"I want a blood sample."

"Good God, why?"

"A sick body is sometimes a sick mind. Your physical condition is important."

"I'm not sure I want amateurs taking blood samples from me."

"I'm a nurse." She unbuttoned my jacket and started helping me out of it. "You may not be aware of it, but the V.D. rate among people in our age group is climbing to fantastic heights."

I let her take my blood, my blood pressure, my temperature. After that, we looked into a complicated machine which had eye holes at both ends. From my end I could see pictures flashed by a slide projector. From her end, she could see my eyes and measure the contraction or dilation of my pupils. There were naked girls in erotically stimulating positions, and naked men in what I guessed were supposed to be erotically stimulating positions.

"Flip it back to the fake redhead with long legs and big—"

She snapped the machine off. "You're hopelessly normal."

"My pupils get bigger viewing the girls, remain the same with the men, right?"

She smiled wryly. "They get very big viewing the girls."

"That means I like girls."

She sighed. "I had a strange feeling that you did even before you were tested."

She gave me a date for my first instruction class, writing it on a slip of paper as a reminder, and we then left the laboratory. The crowd backstage had thinned, but Bold-Jepson was surrounded by a group of eager women. Nearby Christiana Bold-Jepson stood sharing him with a tight smile.

Catching sight of us, he broke through the group and came over.

Marianna melted into dazed adoration. "Dr. Bold-Jepson, I'd like to introduce Larry Howe, who has pledged to become one of us."

He held out his hand. "Larry and I have met." He studied me quizzically. "Nicked you for twenty-five, did she?"

Taking his hand I said, "Twenty-six seventy-five, to be exact."

He smiled. "The Lord's work is costly." He turned to the girl. "He can afford it, Marianna. He works for an insurance company so rich they can lose ten million dollars without batting an eye."

"I think there is an eye or two being batted."

This was all beyond Marianna. She just stood, smiling.

He squeezed my arm. "Welcome to C.E.A., Larry. I hope, ah, I hope you are sincere. If you're not, it's, ah, your loss. Isn't it?"

I felt a little guilty. "I like your church," I said, quite honestly.

I was a half hour late getting to Isabel's. We went out for a late snack, and I asked if she thought our sex life was everything it should be, as I wouldn't want to be in the position of having lied on the questionnaire. She thought it over and decided it was okay, considering the job I had, and the irregular hours. She was fascinated by Bold-Jepson's church and wanted to attend with me.

"It's really sort of a bore," I said. It would be a snowy day in August before I exposed her to Bold-Jepson.

We went to my place and listened to some records. And other things, including our respective heartbeats.

At dawn I left for Swigatchit. On a long straight stretch I had the Porsche up to a hundred and ten. The same damned cop came howling up behind me. You can't win.

"I thought you never chased anyone going a hundred."

"For you, I made an exception."

4

Dr. Schoenfield was in a nasty humor. He had dropped his upper partial plate onto the tile floor of the bathroom, rendering it useless for either chewing or conversation.

"There is no doubt that the deceased died from drowning," he said, lisping slightly. "But there's also no doubt in my mind that this death by drowning was assisted."

Barnes leaned forward.

"An examination of the deceased's stomach contents revealed the presence of wild mushrooms. While we shall need further laboratory tests to establish it conclusively, I can say tentatively that the deceased ingested a deadly poison present in the species Amanita phalloides. The deceased had suffered cramps in the limbs, and convulsions, and there is marked deterioration of the red blood corpuscles. All indicate this type of poisoning."

Sergeant Marino whistled softly between his teeth.

"In other words, drowning was due directly to his being made helpless by cramps and convulsions?" asked Barnes.

"This is my considered opinion."

I groaned. "He picked the damned things."

Barnes looked at me. "He picked them?"

"That's what he told me at the cookout. He said, 'I've picked wild mushrooms for years without a single fatality.' "

Marino lit a cigarette. "If he picked them, then there is no change in the situation. An accident."

"If these were the mushrooms served at the cookout, others would have been affected," said Barnes.

I said, "I don't think anyone else ate them. I heard people turning them down right and left. In fact, Bentinck Bold warned me not to eat any."

"Bold steered you away from them?"

I nodded. "He told me they tasted horrible."

"They did," said Barnes.

"*You* ate some?"

"A bite or two. They were so saturated with Tabasco I found them unpleasant."

Dr. Schoenfield smiled, revealing some awkward gaps in his upper teeth. "If you had a bite or two, you should be a pretty sick man. Even dead. A little phallin goes a long way."

Barnes looked a shade whiter. "A bite or two?"

He nodded. "Very dangerous stuff."

Barnes looked sicker. I reviewed the various pharmaceuticals I carry. What antidote would I prescribe for imagined phallin poisoning? I decided one placebo pill and one tranquilizer would do as well as anything. If you give Barnes only one pill, he has no confidence in it.

Schoenfield relented. "Cheer up. If you had ingested phallin, symptoms would probably have shown up long before now."

"Would have *probably* shown up," said Barnes, uncomforted.

Marino scraped his chair back and stood up. The four of us made his small office a bit crowded. I moved to let him get out from behind his desk.

"I've got to start checking everybody who was at the cookout. If anyone else ate the mushrooms—"

"They may be dead," said Barnes, long-faced.

"Or very sick," said Dr. Schoenfield.

All the way back to the Kilgore house Barnes remained in silent communication with his red blood corpuscles, which he was certain were deteriorating rapidly. Dizziness, coupled with an overall faintness; and the two pills hadn't helped.

Barnes went up to his room to lie down. I wandered around looking for Kathryn Kilgore. I found her sunning herself by the pool, wearing a less conservative white bikini, which complemented her tanned body and lustrous black hair better than her mourning bikini.

We chatted a bit about the startling news, which she had already heard from Marino. Marino had telephoned. He had wanted to be sure he had the complete list of guests and help at the cookout.

"I hope I didn't forget anybody," she said.

"Are you certain the mushrooms served at the cookout were picked by your husband? I mean, that they were all wild?"

"Of course they were. He always picked them. He was a mushroom aficionado. He loved the damned things."

"Oh."

"He wouldn't have dreamed of letting us order commercially grown mushrooms."

"Did you ever eat the wild mushrooms he picked?"

She glanced at me, wrinkling her nose. "Do I look like a nit? Of course not. I don't even like regular mushrooms."

"With all his experience," I said, "do you think it would be possible for him to make such a deadly mistake?"

She reached for a cigarette. "You only make one mistake with those damned things." I lit it for her. "There was that famous chef a few years ago. He had been picking wild mushrooms all his life. I showed the article to Ossie. He just snorted."

"Still, it seems strange that—"

"Besides, he was drunk as a skunk when he went out to pick them."

I took off my jacket. It was too warm in the sun.

"Ossie used to stay stoned for four or five days when he finished a book. The only thing he had for breakfast Saturday morning was a pitcher of bloody marys. Then he went out mushroom gathering."

I leaned back and closed my eyes.

"I said to him, 'How do you expect to tell a mushroom from a toadstool when you're blind drunk?' "

"What did he say?"

"He slapped me. The clod." She sighed. "I suppose the estate will be sued for millions if anyone else is sick, or dies."

I found Barnes in the library reading up on mushrooms. Kilgore had at least a dozen volumes on the subject, most of them lavishly illustrated with full-color plates showing thousands of varieties.

"Might as well let it be," I said. "Ossie not only picked them, he was drunk as a skunk when he did so. According to widow Kathryn."

Barnes laid down the book, then felt the pulse in his wrist for a minute. "Do I look a little pale to you?"

"No."

"I feel as though I look a little pale."

"Why don't you try looking, instead of feeling?"

"Don't be smart-ass. I'm in no mood for it."

"Okay. I just want to know, why don't we go back to New York?"

Barnes sighed. "Because I'm not satisfied with the case."

"What the widow Kathryn said can probably be verified by the servants."

Barnes consulted his cigarette notebook, then thrust it back into his pocket angrily. It had said "no-no." "He most probably did pick them. This does not preclude someone else picking some too."

"Oh, come on."

"It would be a fairly foolproof way of collecting ten million dollars. Practically the perfect crime."

I shook my head sadly.

"Why not? Anyone familiar with Kilgore's hobby could easily slip some Amanita phalloides into the batch." He rubbed his forehead wearily. "And know that it would be damned near impossible to prove."

"It's just so preposterous," I said.

"Being insured for ten million dollars is preposterous to begin with."

When we assembled for cocktails before dinner, I was surprised to find Upton Eads with his wife, Susan, still there. Eads was in a much better humor, possibly because it was now known that Kilgore had named him executor of the estate. The others were subdued, even faintly hostile.

"This is absolutely filthy Scotch," said Christiana Bold-Jepson. "Isn't there any Black Label?"

"No, dear, we're all out of Black Label," said Kathryn. "I'm *so* sorry."

"Don't be rude, dear. It's perfectly good Scotch, said the Reverend Bold-Jepson. He looked tired and somewhat hung over.

"How would *you* know?" she asked.

Bentinck sighed deeply. "Why don't you two cut out this childish quibbling?" He was staring at his sister.

"How long do we have to stay here?" Christiana asked.

"You can go back to New York any time you choose, love," said Bold-Jepson.

Barbara Bold pushed her long, beautiful hair away from one eye and said, "I don't see why all these details concerning the estate and Bold House can't be taken care of in New York."

"Because I prefer to take care of them up here," said Eads jauntily. "As a convenience to the widow."

"They don't have to stay here for my convenience," said Kathryn.

"Then let's say it's for my convenience," said Eads.

"Indeed?" asked Bentinck. I had a feeling that Eads would need a pretty terrific manuscript in hand before he sold anything to Bold House in the future.

Eads stared around at the group with a small, smug smile. "It's extremely interesting," he said, "that Ossie died from eating wild mushrooms."

"Is it?" asked Bentinck, his voice even colder.

"Yes, it's very interesting."

During the silence that followed, Bold-Jepson moved to the bar. "Anyone care for another drink?"

Christiana and Bentinck edged past Eads to join him. "See if there's any other Scotch," said Christiana.

Eads shrugged his shoulders, still smiling. "Okay, then, we'll adjourn this kaffeeklatsch to New York, if Kathryn has no objection." He turned to her. "Do you have any objections?"

"No."

"We'll be needing you there."

"I'll stay on. After the funeral."

Eads nodded. He looked down at his glass and then moved to the bar. "I'll have a bourbon, Reverend Bob, if you would be so kind." He rotated the ice cubes in his glass with one finger, trying for another sip. "Very interesting, wild mushrooms."

5

The only one who wept at the funeral was Susan Eads. I remembered that she had burst into tears at the luncheon table earlier, and wondered if she was the only member of the inner circle who cared for Osborne Kilgore. Or maybe she was just a girl who cried easily.

The undertaking establishment had reserved the largest chapel, and it was filled. There were even some stars of stage, screen, and television there, preening and looking appropriately sad and shocked.

Bold-Jepson seemed preoccupied. He spoke in very general terms about the deceased, praising him for the entertainment he had brought to millions. Kathryn sat through it with a bland, calm look.

On the way out, Bentinck came alongside Barnes and said, "Some of the closer friends are gathering at Kathryn's for a drink. You two are welcome, if you care to come."

Barnes wasn't sure alcohol would go with the phallin in his system which was still eating away at his red blood corpuscles, but he decided that duty should prevail. Marino hadn't been able to locate a single individual, other than Barnes, who had eaten the mushrooms. Most of them had been familiar with Mushrooms Ossie-Tabasco. One taste stayed with you for years.

When Bentinck moved away, Barnes said, "They just want to know when they can expect to see their checks."

"I'd like to see a check for five million dollars."

Barnes shook his head. "I haven't even submitted my report yet."

"Why not?"

He glanced at me. "I'm still being gnawed by a hunch that all is not as it should be. Let them wait a few days. Paying out ten million dollars is a serious business."

Kilgore's spacious penthouse overlooked the East River. It was only moderately crowded, a comfortable cocktail party with room to move around. The hors d'oeuvres were sumptuous and varied. Lobster, beluga caviar, Polish ham, huge shrimp, Brie cheese, and other delicacies made this funeral feast the most impressive I had ever attended. Of course, I hadn't attended many, but I had a feeling this would remain number one. Three bartenders and numerous waiters kept the drinks moving with incredible efficiency. No one waited for a refill.

Barnes, who had no appetite, viewed my gourmandizing with barely concealed impatience. He finally stomped off to the terrace. Loading my platter, and snatching a stein of Löwenbräu, I followed him.

Big enough to accommodate a tennis court, the terrace made the crowd seem even thinner. It was carpeted with artificial turf, cool dark green in color, and tastefully decorated with potted plants, flowerboxes, ferns, and other growing things. But *big*. Ossie had liked things big. Big meals, big drinks, big books, big houses. For New York, the terrace was the equivalent of the King Ranch.

Barnes was chatting with Bentinck Bold. As I approached, Bentinck looked at me, nodded, and then turned back to Barnes. "Do you have any idea when Wickersham is going to settle this thing?"

Barnes smiled. "Soon, probably."

"What good is an estate liquidity policy when payment is held up and the estate remains nonliquid? Eads tells me the Internal Revenue is already after him."

Barnes stared down at the tarnished gray metal of the East River. "The man has been dead less than a week. I seriously doubt that the Internal Revenue—" He paused. "Anyway, that would be Eads's problem, wouldn't it?"

Bentinck grinned. "Obviously, we are looking forward to Bold House's check with considerable anticipation."

Barnes nodded. "I would imagine so." He thought for a few seconds. "The only thing I can suggest is that you telephone Dale Jones. I doubt, however, that he will give you a definite answer, since he hasn't received my report. Of course, we have discussed the case at great length."

"You mean he's waiting for *your* recommendation?"

"Probably."

"So what are you waiting for?"

"To decide what to recommend."

Bentinck frowned. "What possible reservations could you have?"

Christiana Bold-Jepson came up, looking flushed. "I'm leaving, Ben," she said, "I've just about had it with Kathryn."

Kathryn approached, walking rapidly. "You really should pull yourself together, Chris."

Chris stared at her, unblinking. Then she quickly tossed the contents of her glass in Kathryn's face, dropped the glass, and walked away.

Kathryn stood, too startled to speak. Bentinck quickly handed her his spotless white handkerchief, shaking his head apologetically. Kathryn dabbed her face. "That girl really needs help, Ben."

"It would be a big help if you'd lay off of Bob," he said.

She finished wiping her face. "Bob's been in the public domain for some time."

Bold-Jepson came up. "What's all the brouhaha?"

"Chris just threw her drink in my face."

"Oh." He rubbed his chin. "Oh my."

He gave me a worried look and hurried away. Bentinck took Kathryn's arm and walked her out of earshot.

Barnes looked smug. Marriage is just one big battle, as far as he is concerned, and he's glad he's well out of it.

Eads strolled over. "Our widow got sloshed. Literally, that is."

Barnes smiled politely, then stared down at the river again.

"When is Wickersham going to pay our claim? The damned policy was taken out so the estate would be liquid. Instead, it's all tied up, nonliquid, and as executor *my* hands are tied."

"Only time will tell," said Barnes.

"What the hell kind of an answer is that?"

Barnes turned to him with a stern look. "It's the only answer I can give you at the moment."

"Are you going to force us to take legal action?"

"I wouldn't advise it."

Eads sipped his drink. "Why not?"

"That route could take months. I expect you'll have some kind of definite answer from Wickersham in a few days."

Eads nodded, his face suddenly contorted in a look of ecstatic surprise. "Ummmmm, *ummmmm*," he said, as though someone had just presented him with a platter of finger-licking fried chicken. Then he keeled over, his drink and ice cubes tumbling over the Astro-turf.

There was a doctor in the building, but locating him and persuading him to come up to the penthouse took almost as long as the arrival of the police ambulance. He was at least able to pronounce Eads dead.

Throughout the confused fifteen minutes, Susan had remained kneeling beside her husband, calm and dry-eyed. At first she had tried mouth-to-mouth resuscitation, then given up when it was obvious that it was having no effect. It was not until the doctor arrived that she would let Bentinck help her to her feet.

Barnes, who had bent over Eads, loosening his tie and collar, and had then been superseded by Susan, was looking white and shaken.

"Heart attack?" I asked, keeping my voice very low.

Barnes shook his head. "I'm not a doctor. For what it's worth, I'd say no."

"Would you like a couple of Bufferin?"

"No." He rubbed his forehead wearily. "I may be making a complete ass of myself, but I'm going to call Shunk."

Lieutenant Shunk of Homicide was our old friend-enemy. Barnes's friend, my enemy. I watched Barnes head for the telephone with a certain amount of confusion. The shock of watching a man die who had been talking to us so forcefully only seconds before had unnerved me more than I realized. The thought of murder hadn't entered my mind. It still seemed a bit far-fetched.

Kathryn came up, looking distraught. "I just can't believe it. It's just *impossible*."

Barbara Bold had her arm around Susan Eads, comforting her. Susan was staring at the terrace floor, saying nothing. I thought perhaps she was too shocked to cry. Bentinck whispered something to Barbara, and the two guided Susan back into the apartment.

"He was so buoyant and healthy, I wouldn't have *dreamed*—" said Kathryn.

I couldn't think of any comment to make, and looked around. My virtually untouched platter of lobster salad, Polish ham, and other goodies was still on the outdoor table where I had placed it hurriedly. What a waste. I not only had no appetite now, but couldn't have eaten it if I had, since it would somehow be very poor form. Drinking, however, was not taboo. I had noticed several people hurrying to the bar for stiff ones.

"I think I'll go to the bar and have a drink. Medicinal."

She looked at me with a small smile. "Shock."

I nodded.

"Everyone is. They all want to leave, but don't know quite whether they should."

The bartender eventually got to me. "A double Scotch, please," I said.

"That's the way I'm pouring all of them. Double."

"Good."

"It's a helluva thing. You come back here from a funeral, and have somebody else drop dead."

"Yeah." I sipped my drink, brooding about death and time. I read somewhere that atomic clocks are so accurate because the cesium atom vibrates exactly 9,192,631,770 times a second. What I can't figure is how they count them up that fast? I can see the nine billion, but what about that odd one hundred and ninety-two million, six hundred and thirty-one thousand and seven hundred and seventy vibrations? How can *anything* vibrate nine billion times in one second?

Shunk came bustling in as though he owned the penthouse and was annoyed to see so many people there messing up the clean carpets. He's a big man, almost as tall as Barnes's six foot three. He has curly, taffy-colored hair, dirty green eyes, and a nasty sneer.

"Hello, junior," he said to me, waggling his cheap plastic-tipped cigar. "Don't get in my hair."

"Don't worry. With the dandruff problem you have, you're safe."

The cigar quit waggling. He paused to light it. "Listen, bright eyes, don't give me any more lip. I'm liable to tear off those phony sideburns and stuff them up your nostrils."

My sideburns irritate him. It's not enough that I've given up my extra-long hair and become one of the plastic people. He begrudges me my sideburns and my big mustache.

Barnes nudged him on, gesturing toward the terrace, and they walked on out to examine the now blanket-covered remains of Eads. The cop who was standing guard straightened up and looked nervous when he saw Otto Shunk. Among the group following Shunk I recognized Melvin Phillips from the medical examiner's office.

Phillips whipped the blanket back and bent over Eads. I saw Barnes reach down among the potted plants and retrieve Eads's glass, which he had apparently put there for safe-keeping during the excitement. He handed it to Shunk. Shunk looked at it, sniffed it, and then passed it on to one of the technicians.

After some ten minutes of conferring, Shunk allowed the ambulance men to take the body away. He then called everyone together and requested that they give their names, addresses, and serial numbers to the officers sitting near the door. Then, he suggested, they would probably wish to leave.

The guests began a polite rush to the door, crowding and pushing a little.

I went back to the bar and ordered another Scotch. Bar service had been reduced to one mournful bartender, and the huge room was almost empty.

Kathryn Kilgore was sitting alone in one corner. On a coffee table before her was a bottle of wine and a platter of food heaped higher than the one I had left on the terrace. She was eating rapidly and surreptitiously, as though someone might be creeping up from behind to snatch the food away from her.

6

"Now we're getting somewhere," said Barnes, looking almost cheerful, which is unusual for him, because he worries a lot. We were sitting in Shunk's office, and Shunk was looking as mean as ever. The autopsy report on Eads was lying on his desk. Eads had not succumbed through natural causes. He had received an unhealthy dose of aconite. Not in his drink, however. Pure Jack Daniel's and branch water.

"Don't let it go to your head," said Shunk, "Eads could have been killed for some other reason."

Barnes raised his eyebrows. "That would be stretching coincidence pretty far, wouldn't it? He was threatening somebody in the group when he said it was very interesting that Ossie had died from eating wild mushrooms. The next time the whole group is together, someone slips him an aconite mickey."

"They are not necessarily connected," said Shunk. "The man was murdered. That could be the reason, or there could be a totally unconnected reason. A good cop doesn't jump to conclusions."

Barnes stood up. "You're absolutely right, Otto. You should investigate all possibilities. As it happens I'm only interested in the possibility that affects my client, and that's the possibility that Kilgore was murdered by one of the beneficiaries."

Shunk leaned back and stared at the ceiling. "Keep me

fully informed," he said; then, lowering his eyes to me, he added, "and that includes you, junior."

I started to tell him that if he kept on calling me "junior" I would report to him in words of two, three, and even four syllables, making it very difficult for him. I decided against it. Needle Shunk too far and his blood pressure rises dangerously.

In the long wasteland of Broadway that stretches from City Hall north to Fourteenth Street, Eamon Berkowitz has his workshop. If Eamon had stuck with the I.R.A., he would probably now be the second Jewish Lord Mayor of Dublin. Instead he chose to stay in the United States and make a fortune putting together ultra-sensitive electronic devices. In a shabby loft building in what is probably the shabbiest business section of New York, his overhead is very low. His prices are very high. They say a lot of the difference goes to Israel.

"Eamon, I need some more tape recorders," said Barnes. "Two, very small and top quality."

Eamon is a big man with immaculate gray hair and an Honest Abe Lincoln face. He still speaks with the brogue of the country he left many years ago. "Now that'll be costing you," he said, smiling. "How small would you be wanting them to be?"

"Small enough to carry unobtrusively in a jacket pocket."

Eamon laughed. "Now I thought you were wanting something small, like the pea under the princess's mattresses. Would you say, a little larger than a cigarette package, king-size?"

Barnes nodded. "Fine."

"Now that'll be no problem."

"How much?"

He did some quick figuring on a scratch pad. "Fourteen thirty-five for the two."

He didn't mean fourteen dollars and thirty-five cents.

"I need them in a big hurry."

"Add a hundred dollars. I'll keep some of my people on overtime tonight."

"When can I get them?"

Eamon scratched his chin. "Say half-twelve tomorrow?"

Barnes nodded. "Good."

We shook hands and then started picking our way through the cluttered rooms to the freight elevator, Eamon accompanying us. "I never ask my customers questions," he said, "but I can't help be wondering what you're up to this time."

Barnes grasped his arm, smiling. "It's going to be an interesting experiment. I'll tell you about it someday."

Eamon pulled open the elevator door for us. "Good. We'll share a jar, Berkeley Barnes, and talk up a storm." He pronounced it 'Barkly,' reminding me of Dale Jones.

We went back to our offices in the Pan Am building. Barnes has an office. I have a closet. He maintains I'm too young to have claustrophobia. When I protested that age had nothing to do with it, he pointed out that if I can stand riding in an elevator, I can stand my office, which is about that size.

Fortunately I spend most of my time in Barnes's office, which is large and comfortable. I stretched out on the big leather sofa while he called Sergeant Marino, and listened again to him expounding his theory that Osborne Kilgore had been murdered. From the conversation I gathered that Shunk had already been in touch with Marino, and that Marino had reopened the case.

Immediately following Kilgore's autopsy, Marino had tried, in a somewhat perfunctory way, to investigate the possibility of a secret wild-mushroom picker. Someone who might have added lethal Amanita phalloides to Ossie's harmless harvest. He hadn't had much luck. No one had seen anyone other than Kilgore skulking around with wild mushrooms. Two of the servants had noticed Kilgore when he brought back his large basket of freshly picked crop. The basket had remained in the kitchen for several hours until Kilgore had used the contents at the cookout. Marino admitted that anyone in the house could have wandered into the kitchen and deposited a few Amanita phalloides in the basket, but at the time it had not seemed likely.

Now with Eads dead, an obvious victim of a murderer who was probably also present at the cookout, the possibility was much more interesting. Marino promised Barnes he would backtrack, cover the same ground thoroughly and in more detail.

"You haven't mentioned why we particularly need tape recorders," I said. Ordinarily we didn't tape, and when we did it was done openly, with a regular tape recorder.

"That's right, I didn't, did I," he said, and picked up the phone to call his friend Hank Blomberg in the District Attorney's office.

He can be aggravating that way. One of these days maybe I'll hand him a pep pill when he needs a tranquilizer and watch him fret himself into a frenzy. Actually I couldn't do it. Even as an unlicensed and unwilling physician I subscribe to the oath of Hippocrates.

Barnes finished brainwashing Blomberg on the Kilgore-Eads situation and hung up. "Now," he said, "you want to know why we need tapes. First, I want to give you some pertinent background information. I've been working while you've been loafing."

"Relaxing, call it," I said, sitting up.

"While you've been loafing, unable to concentrate upon anything more serious than Miss Ding-Dong."

He can't get over Isabel's last name being Bell. "Isabel is as serious as I want to get."

He shuffled some papers on his desk, eyeing me sternly. I could see one of his terse summaries coming up and tried to look especially alert.

"As far as Wickersham's interests are concerned, we have five possibilities. One, that Kathryn Kilgore may have killed her husband. Two, that Bentinck Bold may have killed him. Three, that Christiana Bold-Jepson may have killed him. Four, that either Barbara Bold or the Reverend Bold-Jepson might have done it to help his or her mate. Five, that Kilgore's murder might have resulted from a conspiracy involving both beneficiaries."

I scratched my head. "Or six, maybe Hal Zimmerman did it so he wouldn't have to edit another Kilgore manuscript."

Barnes laughed. "I'm grateful that this won't be Wickersham's problem. Zimmerman has only a token amount of stock in Bold House."

"Maybe someone totally unconnected with the insurance did it."

"Possible."

"But you're mainly interested in seeing that Wickersham doesn't have to pay out."

He gave me an annoyed look. "Don't be childish. We're being paid by Wickersham to investigate the possibilities that affect Wickersham's business. Any gratuitous help we can give Shunk or Marino, fine."

"Okay."

"Our job is to find out whether any of the five people benefiting from the policy had anything to do with it. If they didn't, Wickersham pays, and we go on to another job. Hopefully."

"Okay."

"Why did you bring it up, anyway?"

I hadn't meant to question Barnes's integrity. It would be on a par with suggesting that Chase Manhattan had a policy of short-changing children. "I don't know. I wish I hadn't."

He smiled, then dropped his eyes to his notes for a moment. "Christiana Bold-Jepson owns forty-three percent of Bold House. Bentinck owns the same. The remaining fourteen percent is divided between Zimmerman and three other key employees. Christiana wants to get out. Two million plus would be nice traveling money."

"Why?"

"Why what?"

"Why does Christiana want to get out?"

"My source says she and brother Bentinck are not getting along."

I put my feet up. "What does your source say about Kathryn Kilgore?"

He chuckled. "Your talk with her about mushrooms, well, I suppose at that stage I might have accepted it too."

"Accepted what?"

"Kathryn has a master's degree and is working on her doctorate. In biological sciences. She's a botanist."

That curvaceous, bodacious skunklet.

"Of course, there are many areas of specialization within the subject. She may well have only a cursory knowledge of mushrooms."

"I have a feeling that she would be able to recognize an Amanita phalloides."

"Possible." He slapped his notes together and shoved them in a drawer. "Now, the tape recorders. At this point we have no evidence whatsoever. We may get some help from Shunk in tagging whoever poisoned Eads. I'm not so hopeful of Sergeant Marino. Frankly, I don't know where to begin with regard to Swigatchit. Should we go tramping around up there looking for poison mushrooms? I rather doubt we'll find a comb with Kathryn's fingerprints on it resting helpfully in a patch of Amanita phalloides."

"So doubt I."

"With poison growing on the ground this way, almost anyone reasonably intelligent could find it and use it. A few minutes in a library studying color plates would be sufficient."

He fished out his notebook, consulted it, and decided that a cigarette was permissible. "The only thing we can do is dig relentlessly. We're going to talk to these people until we're blue in the face, if necessary." He lit his cigarette. "We're going to cross examine them as though our lives depended upon it. We're going to find out who's lying and who isn't."

I put my feet down and sat straighter. If we were going to dig relentlessly, and talk ourselves blue in the face too, I might as well face up to it. It could mean no Isabel for several days.

"We're going over and over their stories until discrepancies show up. Is that it?"

"No." He fiddled with his desk calendar, making a quick note. "We're going to experiment with a new technique. Have you heard of psychological stress evaluation?"

I had, but I wasn't sure I understood it completely, or whether it was reliable. It was a new type of lie-detecting equipment which worked entirely through analysis of voice vibrations. "Sure."

"We can't strap Bentinck Bold into polygraph equipment, but we can certainly tape what he says." He puffed on his cigarette for a few seconds. "And then have the tape analyzed."

Why hadn't I thought of that? "Does it really work?"

"Quite a few people say they are getting excellent results with it."

"It detects stress, doesn't it?"

He nodded. "Pretty much the same as a polygraph. Except that all you need is a tape of the voice."

With a polygraph you certainly couldn't test anyone secretly. There was the blood-pressure cuff on the arm, the accordion hose around the stomach to measure respiration, and two electrodes to hold. I remembered a descriptive phrase. "Muscle microtremors."

Barnes nodded. "When people are under stress the normal inaudible frequency modulation vibrations disappear completely. Without stress, they are present. There may be no noticeable difference in the actual sound of the voice, whether under stress or completely relaxed."

"Of course the tapes won't be admissible in court."

"No. But can you imagine any of that crew, Bentinck Bold, Kathryn, or the reverend agreeing to a regular lie-detector test?"

"Nope."

The possibilities were endless and fantastic. Secret lie-detection equipment could put politicians out of business right and left.

"You know something," I said, "I didn't even know the voice had *in*audible frequency modulation vibrations."

He smiled. "As a matter of fact, neither did I until recently." His cigarette was getting short, and he crushed it out regretfully. "Between now and tomorrow noon I think we'll put together some questions. Good stress-causing questions."

7

The Upton Eadses lived in a loft in SoHo. Not Soho, London; SoHo, New York City. From my impressions of Eads, I would have expected him to have a house in Larchmont. The plaster walls of the hallway were cracked and grimy, and the worn linoleum floor covering was ready for retirement.

Barnes's plan was that we would each interview everyone importantly connected with the case, then compare tapes and have them analyzed. We would then go back to those requiring a second round. Susan Eads was my first assignment.

I rang the bell. In a moment there was a click and one eye stared at me through the peephole.

"Oh, it's you," she said. "You're—?"

"The man from Wickersham insurance."

"Yes. Of course."

For a few seconds I heard nothing but the clicking and clanking of various locks and bolts being manipulated. Then the door opened, and Susan Eads stood aside for me to come in. Entering, I almost tripped on the police lock. It consisted of a thick metal pole with one end nestled in a steel plate in the floor. The other end was fastened to a plate on the edge of the door. Locked, it leaned tightly against the door, somewhat on the principle of a chair wedged under the doorknob.

"I see you're well fortified," I said.

"Yes," she said. "Look." She pointed out numerous

crowbar and screwdriver marks on the outer edges of the heavy wooden door and frame. Aside from the pry marks, the wood looked as though it had been repeatedly attacked by a demented beaver.

"One day they'll just take an ax to it," she said.

I shook my head. "What do you have here, the Koh-i-noor diamond?"

She closed the door. "No, it's just the times, I guess. And the neighborhood."

Once inside, and away from the door with its bolts and chains and pole, you were immediately in an environment that suggested money. The immense old loft area was an open-plan landscape with plants, bookshelves, and other dividers creating various living and working areas, all but one richly furnished. The exception was a section under a skylight which contained a large easel, drawing board, taboret, framed canvases, model stand, and other equipment of the professional artist. It was simple, uncluttered, and uncarpeted.

"Are you an artist?" I asked.

She nodded. "This was my studio before Upton and I were married. We decided to refurnish it. Instead of buying one of those stupid coops uptown."

"It's impressive."

"Thank you." She led me to an area which would have been a spacious living room if it had had walls. "Sit down. Would you care for coffee, or a drink?"

"Coffee would be great."

Upton had been more adventurous than he had appeared to be. Susan, who was certainly no more than twenty-five, had the sort of sleepy, highly sexed beauty that would have kept him busy warding off younger intruders. I had pictured her as a girl who had married for money, or at least for the glamour of moving in the prestigious Kilgore orbit. Apparently she had a career of her own.

She returned shortly with a small tray containing a coffeepot, two large white mugs, sugar and cream and spoons. She placed it on the coffee table, then joined me on the large sofa, sitting decorously about two feet away.

"Sugar, cream, black?"

"Black, please."

She poured.

"Thank you." I was about to reach for the cup when I felt something moving on my jacket sleeve. I looked down. Sitting there, staring at me with black, bulging eyes, was one of the biggest and hairiest tarantulas I had ever seen. For a second I was petrified, then I jumped up and shook my arm. The tarantula dropped to the floor gracefully and squatted there staring at me, flexing his bent, hairy legs as though about to spring. I raised one foot and was about to stomp when Susan shouted, "Stop! Don't! That's William."

"William?"

"A pet."

"A pet? A *pet*?" I couldn't think of anything else to say.

She eased off the sofa and crawled on her hands and knees over to William. I didn't know which way to look. From that angle Susan was certainly worth watching, but I didn't dare take my eyes off William for more than a second. Spiders and tarantulas panic me.

Susan held her hand flat on the floor, palm up, and gently nudged William. "Poor William, did the nasty man frighten you? Come on, baby, I'll put you back in your house with Tabitha." She waited patiently while William considered the offer. "Come on, William," she cooed, then looking up at me, said, "He's such a timid little fellow."

He didn't look timid to me.

William finally stepped daintily onto her palm. He was so big he could hardly fit. She got carefully to her feet and carried him across the room to a large glass case with a layer of sand and rock on the bottom. She lifted the screened top with one hand and set him gently down inside with the other. "Now, there, the bad man can't get you."

"Get *him*. He tried to get *me*. You should have seen the look in his eyes. He was ready to spring."

She laughed. "He's harmless. You frightened him. He was just exploring you."

I sat down cautiously, still shaken. "You don't, uh, have any more pets around, do you?"

"No, just William, and his mother, Tabitha." She picked up her cup and sipped, smiling. "I sometimes think William is the reincarnation of my first husband. All hairy and tickly all over."

I looked around. "Is, uh, Tabitha—?"

"Safe in the case, where you can't frighten her."

"I would never wish to frighten her."

I drank some coffee. I was so disconcerted I had to stop and think carefully to remember why I was there. I reached in my jacket pocket and activated the tape recorder, coordinating it with a pretended search for matches to light the cigarette she was now holding. I don't smoke, having given up pot. If I stayed around Susan Eads long I might be driven back to it.

She picked up a table lighter and took care of it while I was still looking.

"Sorry," I said. "What, uh, happened to your first husband?" Maybe Tabitha ate him.

She expelled a fair amount of smoke. "He drove head on into a brick building. On his motorcycle."

"Oh. Sorry to hear that," I said, embarrassed. I wouldn't have asked. I had assumed divorce.

"That's all right. He had it coming to him, the bastard." She flicked ashes off her cigarette before there were any to flick. "But you're here to talk about Upton, I know. Have the police found out anything? All they tell me is they are making progress."

I shook my head. "Why did you marry Upton Eads?"

She stared at me. "You mean, because he was so much older? I wanted an older man. I was sick of being beaten and kicked and chewed up by a twenty-year-old hairy monster. After Bill crashed I decided that if I ever married again it would be to an older man, a *gentle* older man."

"Upton Eads didn't impress me as being particularly gentle."

"He was."

"Why do you think he was killed?"

"I think he knew something about Ossie's death."

"You cried at the funeral. You were the only one who did."

"I liked Ossie."

"Liked?"

"Loved him a little, I guess."

"Were you—?"

"Lovers? Why should I tell you?"·

I shrugged. "You don't have to, of course."

"Well, we weren't. Ossie wanted to divorce Kathryn and marry me. I couldn't do that to Upton. I didn't love him the way I had loved Bill, but there was deep affection."

"Kilgore wanted to dump Kathryn? He seemed very jealous. At the cookout."

"Only because she was one of his possessions. He didn't love her."

I drank some coffee and thought a few seconds. "Upton mentioned nothing to you? About his suspicions, or what he saw?"

"No."

"What do you think he knew?"

"I have no idea."

"Do you suppose he saw Kathryn or Bentinck picking mushrooms?"

She shrugged. "Who knows?"

"If this was the reason he was murdered, you may be in grave danger. The murderer may decide you do know something."

She took a deep drag and then crushed out the cigarette. "This has occurred to me."

"Would you like for me to ask Lieutenant Shunk to provide protection?"

"No."

"Why not?"

"Too much of a hassle. I'm not that frightened."

I glanced in the direction of her studio. "What do you paint?"

"Abstract. Some commercial work."

"Did Eads leave you well fixed?"

She smiled. "Upton was not poor. I don't have to work, if that's what you mean."

She sipped her coffee for a time in silence. Then she tucked her legs up on the sofa and turned to me. "I saw you at the church the other night."

I nodded. "I didn't see you."

"Bob is so wonderful. He makes you understand how completely fascinating and good life is."

I nodded again. "Have you been a member long?"

"Three years."

"What plateau are you on?"

She smiled. "Only the second. I'm a dummy when it comes to philosophy."

"The reverend and Ossie didn't get along well."

"No—" She started to say something else but changed her mind and trailed off into silence.

"They hated each other?"

"Well—"

"Didn't they?"

"Sometimes, I guess. Ossie thought it was a phony religion. He said Bob was a con man. How could anyone who *gives* so much be a con man?"

That was a question I couldn't answer. If the reverend was a con man, I suspected he was only partially so. He had seemed completely sincere to me.

"The idea of having tarantulas for pets. Was it yours or Upton's?"

"Mine."

"They are ugly and frightening to the average person."

"I'm not an average person."

"You find them attractive? Cuddly?"

She laughed softly. "What are you, an amateur therapist?"

Upton Eads had been a brave man. Weighing her obvious physical charms on one side and the tarantulas on the other, I believe I would have headed for the door.

"Have you ever picked wild mushrooms?"

Her sultry eyes narrowed. "No."

"Have you ever had occasion to use any medicines containing aconite?"

"No." She swung her feet to the floor and crossed her legs. "I suppose you have to ask these questions for the record, but surely you don't think—"

I sipped my coffee. "As you say, it's only for the record. How did you occupy your time the morning before the cookout? Did you see Ossie when he went to pick mushrooms?"

She thought for a few seconds. "No, actually not until shortly before the cookout. We had breakfast sent up to the room. Later I went for a swim, but Ossie wasn't around the pool."

"Where was Upton?"

"With me most of the time."

"Did Upton know how you felt about Ossie?"

"I don't think so. I hope not." She folded her arms across her chest. "One thing you should understand. Upton was a sweet, kind, generous person. He was also a realist. He used to say, 'One day you'll fall for a young man your own age, and I'll just have to accept it.' "

"It would have been very awkward, though, your falling for Ossie. He was Upton's biggest client."

She thought about that for a while. "Yes, it would have been." She stood up. "I'm sorry to hustle you out, but I have a dentist's appointment. I have to get ready and leave shortly."

I thanked her for the coffee and left, tripping over her burglarproof pole again.

My next stop was Sutton Place. Barnes had given me first go at Kathryn, expressing the probably mistaken theory that "being young, handsome, and virile"—a short laugh to indicate that I'm not all that virile—"you may get more information from her." I'm the type a murderess would go for.

She wasn't particularly glad to see me. On the other hand, she wasn't annoyed. Neutral, say.

I followed her onto the terrace, walking around the ghost of Upton Eads lying on the turf, the way you skirt a grave.

We sat down on a thickly upholstered glider and stared at each other while I surreptitiously started the tape recorder.

"What is it you wish to see me about?"

No coffee? No drink? Oh, well.

"We are working on the theory that your husband may have been murdered."

She tossed her head back and gave a short, unpleased laugh. "Anything to delay paying up, is that it?"

"Not at all. How would you explain Upton Eads's murder?"

She shrugged. "He was an agent, wasn't he? They always have plenty of enemies." She turned and poked my chest with her forefinger. "Did you know that he sold the motion-picture rights to *Chastity O'Toole* for five thousand dollars?"

The picture had grossed ten million so far and was still going strong.

"The author was at my party. Cartwright Tremd. He glared at Upton the whole time."

"Your party?"

She was momentarily embarrassed. "I mean, what would you call it? Ossie's party? When we came back here after the funeral."

"You mean when Eads was poisoned." I glanced at Eads's ghost, still lying out there, not twenty feet away.

She shuddered. "Poisoned. What a horrible word. No one tells me anything."

"The police didn't tell you?"

She glanced up at the blue sky, as though trying to remember. "They were here and asked a lot of questions. I got the impression something was wrong."

"You think Cartwright Tremd poisoned Eads?"

She pointed to her own chest, a very nicely filled out chest indeed, and said, "*I* am not accusing him, of course. I would just say that if I were him, *I* would be in a murderous rage."

"You told me you didn't know anything about wild mushrooms."

"I don't."

"You're a botanist, and you don't know anything about mushrooms?"

She tucked her head down and glanced at me, half smiling. "It's a vast subject. I've never been particularly interested in mycelia."

"What?"

"Fungi."

"Oh."

I wondered what the stress evaluator would say to that. It could be one of those half truths that might not cause much stress.

"You say you've *never* picked mushrooms."

"Certainly not."

"Never?"

"Not that I can remember. My father was a botanist. We used to go out collecting specimens all the time, but I don't recall ever picking mushrooms."

"You wouldn't be able to tell the difference between Amanita phalloides and an edible mushroom?"

"No." She hesitated. "I mean, not offhand. I'd have to consult one of Ossie's books."

"And you haven't done so?"

"No."

"I've heard rumors that Ossie wanted to divorce you."

Her small mouth hardened. "One hears all kinds of rumors."

"He didn't?"

"Of course not. You saw the kind of scene he made because of a harmless swim I had with Bob. If he wanted to divorce me he wouldn't have cared."

"I don't see that. Suspected infidelity is what breaks up most marriages."

She pointed to her magnificent chest again. "*I'm* the one who had grounds for divorce."

"He was unfaithful?"

"Frequently."

"Who with?"

"Most recently, Susan Eads."

"Can you prove it?"

"No."

"Did Upton know?"

"I have no idea."

"Whoever put the Amanita in with the other mushrooms must be a monster. She or he could have killed a dozen people."

She looked away. "No one did. Ossie picked them by mistake."

"We don't believe that. The police don't believe that."

She glanced back at me. "Anyway, no one ever ate Ossie's awful mushrooms."

"Barnes did. He could have died."

She turned and pointed her finger at me again. "You, your attitude is insulting." The finger arced and pointed in her direction again. "*I* don't have to talk to you. I don't care whether your crummy insurance company pays the money or not. *I* have an estate worth more than fifteen million dollars coming to me."

I gave her my best sneer. It's one I've copied from Barnes. "Enough for you and Bold-Jepson to live happily ever after on."

She jumped up. "Please leave," she said tightly. "This conversation is ended."

I stood up. "Will you please state unequivocally, yes or no, did you put poisoned mushrooms in your husband's concoction?"

She glared at me. "No," she said quietly. "I did not."

I left, again stepping around poor Eads. I shouldn't have

made Kathryn so angry. Barnes would have some problems with his interview.

Barbara Bold I would have gladly interviewed on my own time. Next to Isabel, she would be the chick I would most like to get twin tattoos with.

The Bentinck Bolds lived in a renovated old townhouse on East Nineteenth Street. Flanked by run-down rooming houses of the same shape and vintage, I guessed the Bold house had taken plenty of renovating. There were two nameplates in the vestibule, "Bentinck Bold" on one, and "Robert Bold-Jepson" and "Christiana Bold-Jepson" on the other. At least his name was on top of hers.

Barbara Bold answered the door herself, looking harassed as well as beautiful. She pushed her lovely hair aside with the back of her hand and said, "Oh, it's you."

"May I come in and talk to you for a minute?"

She hesitated. "I really think you should talk to Bentinck. Go to the office and talk to Bentinck."

"Barnes is talking to Bentinck."

She smiled. "I see. I rate the assistant."

"Well—"

"Oh come on in. Things are in a mess. This is fixit day."

"Fixit day?"

"There's a man fixing the television set, for one. Another man is fixing the washer, and a *third* man is fixing the elevator. It's a miracle that they all came at once, and at the time they said they would come."

We walked through the living room, where a body lay motionless behind the television set. I could only see his legs, but I could have sworn he was asleep.

"For goodness' sake, did everything bust at once?"

"We'd better go in Bentinck's study. Nothing in there is being repaired. Yet." She turned and spoke over her shoulder. "No, everything didn't bust at once. It's taken a month to get someone here for the washer, two weeks for the television man, and a week for the elevator repairman. Chris and Bob are getting pretty sick of walking up all those steps."

73

"They have the top floors?"

"Four and five. We made those two floors into an apartment for them."

Bentinck's study was a large room at the back of the house, overlooking a patio and nicely tended garden. It was comfortable with somewhat worn leather furniture and floor-to-ceiling bookshelves covering two walls.

"Even at that we have more room than we need, with the basement and three floors. Please sit down."

I slumped into a big, overstuffed leather chair and stretched my legs out, admiring her as she sat down primly on a sofa across from me and adjusted her short skirt to avoid overexposure.

"What do you want to talk about?"

"The police are beginning to think Kilgore was murdered."

She nodded slowly. "Bentinck will be furious."

"Because of further delay in paying the insurance claim?"

She looked past me. "Yes, of course."

"What do you think?"

"About Ossie's death? I think he picked them by mistake."

"Then why was Eads killed?"

She shook her head. "Who knows?"

A short, fat, dark-haired man appeared in the doorway. "Lady, you got to come down and look. You ain't got no pump in this washer."

She got up. "Excuse me," she said, and, walking toward the door, yelled, "The other man took the pump away this morning."

From the hall I could hear his voice. "Lady, I can't fix no washing machine when it ain't got a *pump.*"

"But it's *your man* who took the pump away, dammit."

Their voices grew indistinct as they headed for the basement. I pried myself out of the deep chair and strolled around, looking at the framed photographs on the two walls that had windows and no bookshelves. Most of them were pictures of Bentinck. Bentinck and the Mayor. Bentinck and the Governor. Bentinck and a famous actress. Bentinck and a Nobel Prize winner.

One frame held a citation. Medal of Honor. "Bentinck Bold, 2nd Lieutenant, Infantry, did blah, blah, blah, his position overrun, did singlehandedly kill eleven of the enemy, blah, blah, then wounded in one leg did crawl a hundred yards to an enemy bunker and cleaned it out, killing eight more of the enemy—" Wow! I quit reading. Ever try to crawl a hundred yards, even without being wounded? It's tough, man. I did enough of it in Vietnam to know. I never killed nineteen of the enemy, which is probably just as well. We just crawled and crawled, and wriggled and wriggled, and the only times we saw any of the enemy it always turned out to be South Vietnamese. From the date on Bentinck's citation it was obvious that it applied to the Korean War.

On a table in a corner I found a large scrapbook. It was filled mainly with press clippings. Bentinck heading a commission for the Mayor, Bentinck addressing a committee of publishers, Bentinck accepting the chairmanship of a charity drive. One item, tucked toward the back, was headlined, "MUGGERS ATTACK 'VICTIM'; HE SENDS THREE TO THE HOSPITAL." I read the story, smiling. Bentinck was one rough hombre when aroused. Not a guy to mess with. Three tough types with switchblades had jumped him, ripping his pockets open. When the dust settled, the three were on the pavement, with various wounds and fractures, and Bentinck was calmly asking a passerby to get the police while he saw that they didn't get away. As it turned out, they weren't going anywhere except to the hospital.

Barbara Bold returned, looking flustered. "These people are really crazy. He's blaming *me* because there's no pump in the washing machine, when *his* man took the pump away!"

I nodded sympathetically. "I was just reading your husband's Medal of Honor citation."

She sat down, still looking unhappy. "Bentinck was a very mixed-up guy in those days. Of course, it was long before we met." She stared in the direction of his desk. "After he got out of the hospital, his leg was too bad for combat. He volunteered for a bomb-disposal unit. He spent the rest of his service defusing tremendous bombs."

"Hmmmm."

"I've often wondered if he had some subconscious drive toward self-destruction."

Bentinck was certainly not the kind of guy who ducked violence. At times he must have welcomed it. But poisoning would not be his bag.

"How did Bentinck get in the publishing business?"

She looked a little startled, then smiled. "Oh, you wouldn't remember. Some years ago he wrote a tremendously successful war novel. They made a horrible movie of it called *Killers Six*."

I'd seen it on television. "Oh, sure."

"Well, after all the taxes came out, he still had a modest stake. Chris put in some money and they started in a small way."

"He's done very well."

She looked away. "Yes, he has."

"I hear Chris wants to break up the partnership."

She glanced back at me, startled. "Where did you hear that?"

"Just a rumor Barnes heard."

"I can't imagine—"

"It isn't true?"

"No. But if it were, I can't see that it would be any business of yours."

I smiled, hoping she would consider it an apology. "Wickersham is interested in anything and everything concerning a company they're paying five million dollars to."

She was still angry. "That doesn't give them the right to spread rumors that might hurt Bold House."

I shook my head. "Barnes is very discreet. He wouldn't tell you what time it is unless he was certain you had a right to know. He's the last person to spread a rumor."

Another repairman, this one a gawky youth, tall and blond, stuck his head in the door.

"Ma'am, I got your picture nice and clear, colors just right. You wanna look?"

She jumped up. "For God's sake, there was nothing wrong with the picture. It's the sound we're having trouble with."

He scratched his head. "I thought—is that right? Well, whatta ya know—"

"Excuse me," she said, and left the room muttering.

I was beginning to think I should come back when it wasn't fixit day. I wandered over to the back windows and stared down at the patio and the small, carefully nurtured shrubbery. It occupied an area no more than twenty by twenty-five feet. Contrasted with Kathryn's ballpark it was a postage stamp, but in its charm, much more inviting. Maybe it was because I could picture Barbara Bold having her breakfast there on a sunny Sunday morning.

She returned, still silently talking to herself.

"Now, where were we?"

I said, "For the record I must ask, do you suspect anyone other than Kilgore of picking the poisonous mushrooms?"

"No."

"Do you know definitely who picked those mushrooms, other than Kilgore?"

"No."

"Did you ever pick any mushrooms?"

She smiled. "Certainly not."

"Do you suspect anyone of poisoning Upton Eads?"

"No."

"Do you know definitely who poisoned Eads?"

"No."

"Did you poison Upton Eads?"

"No." She shifted restlessly. "Why would I want to poison poor Upton?"

I shrugged. "Who knows? Maybe he saw Bentinck picking mushrooms."

She stared toward the windows, annoyed. "This is really ridiculous. If Bentinck killed anyone, he wouldn't be sneaky about it."

That was a funny way of putting it, but it summed up my own thinking.

"You mean, he'd just bash them?"

She turned back to me. "Only in self-defense."

I started to speak but stopped. She was holding up her hand. Muffled cries were coming from the hall.

"Sounds like someone calling for help," I said.

We got up and headed in the direction of the noise, which was at the front end of the hall.

The elevator door was wide open on an almost empty shaft. About six inches of the elevator was visible at the top of the opening. A nose and one human eye peered at us through the small space between the elevator floor and the top of the door frame. The eye was very angry.

"Lady, you oughta send this crapped-up elevator back to Outer Mongolia where it was probably made."

"What's the matter?"

"What's the matter? I'm stuck here between floors, that's what's the matter." The nose twitched violently.

"Oh."

"So would you kindly quit standing there and call my company and tell them to send somebody?"

She stared at the eye. "Can't you get out the top?"

"Lady, this elevator don't open on top, unless you happen to be carrying a hacksaw in your hip pocket. *I don't have any hacksaw.*"

"Would you like some water or something?"

The nose twitched again and then emitted a loud sigh. "Lady, why would I want water or something?"

She looked up at him with round-eyed innocence. "Well, I thought, you know, it took you a week to get here. It may be several days before they get around to sending somebody."

The eye closed in patient resignation. "Lady, don't play fun and games with me. Call my company and *get me out of this crapped-up elevator*!

I said goodbye as she headed for the phone. The TV guy would probably electrocute himself before the day was over, and if the fat guy got caught in the washing machine, I didn't want to be there to hear it.

8

It was nearly six o'clock when I got back to the office. Barnes was there, waiting impatiently.

"How did you make out?" he asked.

I collapsed on his big sofa. "Okay, I guess. There were a lot of interruptions with Barbara Bold, but, well, you'll be hearing the tape. How did it go with you?"

"Fine." He fiddled with his small tape recorder, removing the tape. "I suppose we'd better get on with it. You listen to mine, and I'll listen to yours, then we'll—"

"Go out for dinner?" I interrupted hopefully.

"Then we'll send out for sandwiches and analyze what we've got, then develop some more areas to be explored tomorrow."

Sandwiches? No dinner? Oh, well.

"Tomorrow's Eads's funeral."

He snapped his fingers. "Oh, hell, that's right."

I handed him my tapes, and he began putting the first one in his big playback machine.

"At that we can use tomorrow to good advantage. I'll have Miller run these through the Dektor PSE, and we can have an evaluation before we go a second round," he said.

I collected his tapes and went to my so-called office to listen.

His first session was with Bentinck Bold, and the interview consumed about twenty-five minutes. I listened to the whole tape carefully. Much of it was small talk. I rewound and listened to it a second time, skipping the small talk and listening to the pertinent sections.

Barnes: Would you mind describing your movements the evening Kilgore died?

Bentinck: What do you mean?

Barnes: Exactly what you did that evening.

Bentinck: Oh. Well, dinner was over about nine. Let me see. (*Pause.*) Barbara and I strolled down to the beach and watched the waves crash in for a while. Then we came back.

Barnes: Did you see Kilgore?

Bentinck: Not until later.

Barnes: When?

Bentinck: (*Pause.*) Ten or after, I would guess. He was sitting out by the pool. I sat down and chatted for a while.

Barnes: Were the two of you alone?

Bentinck: Yes. The others were inside playing bridge or watching television. Or whatever. Barbara went up to our room.

Barnes: How was Kilgore dressed?

Bentinck: (*Long pause.*) Dressed? I'm not sure I would remember. Let me see. Shorts, moccasins, sport shirt? I think.

Barnes: What did you talk about?

Bentinck: His forthcoming book. We still don't have a good title. (*Pause.*) We were kicking around possible titles.

Barnes: He had just completed this manuscript?

Bentinck: Yes.

Barnes: At lunch the following day you mentioned that Zimmerman must be relieved at not having to edit another Kilgore manuscript. Yet it would seem that there is one in need of editing?

Bentinck: (*Long pause.*) As a matter of fact, Hal wasn't going to edit this one. Ossie had hired another editor to do it on a freelance basis.

Barnes: Why?

Bentinck: (*Long pause.*) Ossie felt that Hal cut out too much of what he considered "good stuff."

Barnes: Did this concern you?

Bentinck: Indeed it did. The man he hired, Fergus Pringle, is a flabby type who would have given in at every point.

Barnes: You might have had a very bad book on your hands?

Bentinck: Yes. (*Loud sigh.*) We decided his reputation could stand one very bad book. He'd be back to Hal when the critics got through with him.

I accelerated the tape through to another section.

Barnes: Have you ever picked wild mushrooms?

Bentinck: No.

Barnes: Do you know of anyone in your group who has, other than Kilgore?

Bentinck: No.

Barnes: Have you ever used medicine with aconite in it?

Bentinck: I didn't even know there was medicine with aconite in it. If I have used any, I am not aware of it.

Barnes: Why do you think Eads was killed?

Bentinck: (*Long pause.*) I must admit it puzzles me. I don't believe it was related to Ossie's death. (*Pause.*) Though I can see you're going to play it for all it's worth to avoid paying ten million dollars.

Barnes: I won't comment on that. Would you mind telling me exactly what you did the morning before the cookout?

Bentinck: Oh, for God's sake. (*Pause.*) I went for a walk in the woods. To pick poison mushrooms, of course.

Barnes: In the interests of expediting this inquiry—

Bentinck: Oh, all right. We woke up, say, about nine-thirty. We had breakfast sent up. I showered and shaved, and then we went for a walk in the woods."

Barnes: You and Mrs. Bold?

Bentinck: Yes. I find that my digestion is better if I take a walk after meals.

Barnes: I do too. Did you see any other members of the group while you were walking?

Bentinck: Yes. Upton Eads.

Barnes: Was he alone?

Bentinck: Yes.

Barnes: Was he carrying anything?

Bentinck: A blackthorn cane. We stopped and chatted for a moment. Then he went up one path and we went up another.

Barnes: Did you notice any mushrooms during your walk?

Bentinck: No.

Barnes: What did you do after you returned from your walk?

Bentinck: I played a couple of sets of tennis with Chris. Then I went for a swim in the pool. I was still there when the other guests started arriving. I went to our room, dressed, and came back down to join the party.

I moved the tape forward to another section.

Barnes: Was Kilgore planning to divorce Kathryn?

Bentinck: (*Pause.*) I couldn't say. They had their ups and downs.

Barnes: It appears that she was, and is, having an affair with Bold-Jepson.

Bentinck: Possible. Gossip doesn't interest me.

Barnes: (*Pause.*) Nor does it interest me. Unless it provides motivation for murder.

Bentinck: Hardly that, I would say.

Barnes: There was deep-seated bad feeling between Kilgore and the reverend on more counts than Kathryn's infidelity.

Bentinck: (*Long pause.*) That's true. (*Pause.*) I suppose you'll dig it out anyway, since it's a matter of public record. Ossie thought Bob was a crook, dishing up a phony religion to con gullible people out of their money. About a year ago he complained to the Attorney General, demanding that the Church of the Expanding Awareness be investigated.

Barnes: And was this investigation made?

Bentinck: Of course. They found nothing even faintly illegal. The church is continually audited by an excellent firm of accountants. Bob takes nothing from the operation but his salary. Which is quite high. But then he deserves it. He works very hard.

Barnes: How high?

Bentinck: Fifty thousand a year.

Barnes: It must have made an awkward situation for you.

Bentinck: Well, yes. However, they more or less patched things up. Our close business and social relationship—

Barnes: A sort of armed truce?

Bentinck: You might call it that.

Barnes: We have learned that Mrs. Bold-Jepson is thinking of pulling her investment out of Bold House.

Bentinck: (*Long pause.*) I can't see that this is any of your business.

Barnes: Under the circumstances, we must consider it our business.

Bentinck: (*Long pause.*) It has nothing to do with the present situation. Chris is a bit fed up with everything, primarily Bob. She is coming to the conclusion that the only happiness she can expect must come through a complete break with the past. She wants to go to Europe to live. Chris is a very fine writer. She wants to work on a book and try to get Bob out of her system.

Barnes: I see.

Bentinck: I've suggested that she just take a leave of absence from the business. We don't want to lose her permanently. Her talent contributes a great deal to the company. (*Pause.*) She loves publishing. Eventually she'd want to come back.

Barnes: And has she agreed to this?

Bentinck: The matter is still being discussed.

I glanced up and saw Barnes standing in the doorway. I shut the machine off.

"This Eads woman. She keeps *tarantulas* for pets?"

I nodded. "Endearing little devils."

He raised his eyebrows.

"One of them, William, was exploring me. I almost stomped him before I found out he was a pet."

"She allows them to roam about, loose?"

"Apparently."

Barnes shook his head. "She must be out of her mind." He gave me a disgusted look and went back to his office.

Barnes is great on pets, being a director of the Anti-Cruelty to Animals Association. He handles all their legal problems free. I could see how having spiders for pets could be an insult to pet lovers the world over. Spiders have very few redeeming features. They operate strictly alone, with no species organization whatsoever. They kill and eat each other, and their mating habits are fairly disgusting. I've read that it isn't true that the female spider always kills the male after mating. It's merely that if she's hungry, and he lingers too long on the scene, she will kill him and eat him. Many males get away.

The next tape was Barnes's interview with Christiana Bold-Jepson. I repeated the procedure, listening to the whole thing, which took about twenty minutes, and then replaying the more important portions.

Barnes: Have you ever picked wild mushrooms?

Chris: On occasion. Not recently.

Barnes: You're familiar with the edible varieties and those which are dangerous?

Chris: I don't consider myself an expert. There are some edible types which are so completely different in color and shape from the poisonous varieties that one is relatively safe in eating them."

Barnes: So I have read.

Chris: Unfortunately the average person's idea of a mushroom is the standard commercially grown types. These have dangerous counterparts with differences small enough to be difficult to detect.

Barnes: You say you haven't picked any mushrooms recently. Exactly what time period is defined by "recently"?

Chris: I can't remember exactly. Certainly more than a year, and never in the vicinity of Osborne Kilgore's place at

Swigatchit. Which should be a concise enough answer for your purposes.

Barnes: Yes. (*Pause.*) Do you know of anyone else, other than Kilgore, who picked wild mushrooms?

Chris: No.

Barnes: Why do you think Eads was killed?

Chris: I haven't the slightest idea.

Barnes: Kathryn is having an affair with your husband.

Chris: (*Pause.*) What else is new?

Barnes: There's the possibility that she wanted to divorce Kilgore and marry Dr. Bold-Jepson. She'd have to give up the Kilgore millions to do it. A fair motive for murder.

Chris: My opinions of Kathryn are obviously prejudiced. So I won't comment on that.

I moved the tape forward.

Barnes: What did you do the morning of the cookout?

Chris: (*Pause.*) Got up late. Had breakfast. Played tennis with Ben.

Barnes: Had breakfast in your room?

Chris: No, on the terrace.

Barnes: Were any others present?

Chris: (*Pause.*) Hal and Debbie Zimmerman.

Barnes: What did you do after you finished tennis?

Chris: Went for a swim.

I yawned and moved the tape forward. I was tired and hungry, and was beginning to think it was a little ridiculous of Barnes not to allow us an hour off for dinner. We had all night to play with the damned tapes. I turned my ears and the recorder back on and listened.

Barnes: What did you do the evening following the cookout?

Chris: (*Pause.*) After dinner I went to our room and read manuscripts.

Barnes: The Reverend Bold-Jepson wasn't with you?

Chris: No. I believe he was playing bridge.

Barnes: You didn't spend a great deal of time together.

Chris: (*Long pause.*) Bob is tremendously attractive to

women. The role of jealous wife is intolerable to me. (*Pause.*) Playing bridge bores me. If I had stayed with the group I would have only been doing it to keep an eye on Bob.

Barnes: I see.

Chris: I don't think you do. But it really doesn't matter.

Barnes: What am I missing?

Chris: I doubt if you would understand anyway.

Barnes: Why not try me?

Chris: (*Long pause.*) Bob and I have had a very wonderful relationship. I can accept that he has an occasional fling with some silly cow at the church. After all, how many men can resist virtually being raped?

Barnes: But you can't accept Kathryn?

Chris: (*Long pause.*) No.

Barnes: You're planning to leave your husband?

Chris: (*Long pause.*) I don't care to talk about it.

Barnes was in the doorway again. "This is taking longer than I thought. Maybe we should take a break and go out for something to eat."

I switched off the tape recorder and stood up. "If you insist," I said, stretching.

"If you'd prefer to send out—"

I grabbed my jacket quickly. "Oh, no, I really need some fresh air." When Barnes buys dinner, it's usually a gourmet's dream, with the check coming to fifty or sixty dollars for two. I'm a gourmet who can't afford it.

We headed east through Grand Central. Well, it wasn't going to be Four Seasons. That was on Park Avenue, north. We left the station and crossed Lexington. There were a lot of good restaurants on Third Avenue.

On Third Avenue he paused in front of a Shillelagh. "Let's just pop in here and have some corned beef and cabbage. I feel like some corned beef and cabbage."

I felt like going on strike. The Shillelagh is a chain of bars. They'll sell you a shot of liquor almost as cheap as you could drink it at home. It was a tragic descent from the possibility of Lutèce or Le Cygne.

Ignoring the look on my face, he pushed on in. We shared a pitcher of beer and ate corned beef sandwiches, since they were fresh out of cabbage. I supplemented this meager dinner with french fries and apple pie, which were not bad. But it was still an insult to a man working overtime.

Barnes was too preoccupied to notice my disenchantment. Fortunately. Had he been able to read my mind, I might have been out of a job.

We went back to our tapes.

Barnes: At the gathering following the funeral, did you notice anyone acting suspiciously, especially with Upton Eads?

Chris: No. What a silly question.

Barnes: Have you any knowledge of medicines containing aconite?

Chris: (*Long pause.*) Yes. My mother suffered from neuralgia. The salve that she rubbed on contained aconite. I remember because the doctor pointed out how dangerous it was. She had to be very careful not to use too much, or use it where there was a break in the skin, or a cut. It's quite deadly.

Barnes: Someone used it on Eads.

Chris: (*Pause.*) Horrible.

Barnes: You have no suspicions with regard to the person who poisoned Eads?

Chris: No.

Barnes: Do you know definitely who poisoned Eads?

Chris: Of course not. I just said no.

Barnes: Did you poison Eads?

Chris: No.

I wound the tape quickly through to the end and removed it. The Reverend Bob was next. After going through the complete tape, I switched back to the most interesting sections.

Barnes: Your relationship with Osborne Kilgore was one

of barely concealed hostility.

Bold-Jepson: That isn't exactly true. We had gotten along reasonably well in recent months.

Barnes: Your romance with Kathryn hardly jibes with that statement.

Bold-Jepson: There is no romance with Kathryn.

Barnes: Considering the scene my associate witnessed, I find this difficult to believe.

Bold-Jepson: I couldn't care less what you believe. I consider our relationship quite casual.

Barnes: Even though it involves sexual intimacy?

Bold-Jepson: (*Pause.*) If it did, it would still be casual. Not "romance."

Barnes: Does it?

Bold-Jepson: That is none of your business. (*Long pause.*) Chris is the only woman I have ever known who didn't bore me after a month or so.

Barnes: But you keep looking.

Bold-Jepson: This is a very peculiar conversation. I can't see how it relates to the Wickersham Insurance Company.

Barnes: We have to consider all the possibilities. One is that Kathryn disposed of Kilgore to open the door to a permanent relationship with you.

Bold-Jepson: This is a shocking thing for you to say. It's ridiculous.

Barnes: You mean, it's not possible that she could feel this strongly about you?

Bold-Jepson: (*Long pause.*) It's unthinkable.

Barnes: There's another possibility you'll also find shocking. This is that you did away with Kilgore so that your wife would be rich, or so that Kathryn would have his complete fortune. Did you kill Osborne Kilgore?

Bold-Jepson: Certainly not. (*Pause.*) My wife is rich enough, thank you. And I have little interest in Kathryn's financial assets.

I cut the sound and moved the tape forward.

Barnes: You went swimming with Kathryn the night before the cookout. What time was this?

Bold-Jepson: (*Pause.*) Somewhere between midnight and one, I believe.

Barnes: Who caught you?

Bold-Jepson: What do you mean?

Barnes: Someone reported your "skinny-dipping" to Kilgore. Who saw you?

Bold-Jepson: I don't know. The pool is visible from some of the rooms in the house. Almost anyone could have seen us.

Barnes: In the dark, from that distance?

Bold-Jepson: The pool is lighted.

Barnes: You were swimming naked in a lighted pool?

Bold-Jepson: Does that shock you?

Barnes: Not if it occurred in a nudist camp. But in a midnight liaison, it smacks of mate switching.

Bold-Jepson: We'll have to drag you into the twentieth century, one way or another. The fact that the lights were on should demonstrate the innocence of our swim to you. Had we planned to make love, we would have turned them off. Neither of us are exhibitionists.

Barnes: I see. (*Long pause.*) Would you describe your movements the morning before the cookout?

Bold-Jepson: (*Pause.*) Let me think. I woke up early, about seven. Went for a swim. In the ocean. Came back, showered, had breakfast.

Barnes: Alone?

Bold-Jepson: Yes. No one else was up. Maggie gave me breakfast in the kitchen. (*Pause.*) After breakfast I sat on the terrace and worked on my sermon. I don't use prepared sermons. (*Pause.*) It's a struggle to say something fresh and meaningful one hundred and four times a year. Two half-hour lectures a week."

Barnes: You give two different sermons every Sunday?

Bold-Jepson: Have to. A great many of our people attend both the morning and evening services.

Barnes: You have a loyal following.

Bold-Jepson: Too loyal.

Barnes: So you worked on your sermons until when?

Bold-Jepson: Until the other guests started arriving.

Barnes: What did you do the evening of the cookout?

Bold-Jepson: After dinner we played bridge. Kathryn and I, Susan and Upton Eads.

Barnes: Were others present?

Bold-Jepson: Hal and Debbie Zimmerman were playing Gin. (*Chuckle.*) He owes her about eight thousand dollars, I think. That girl is some Gin player.

Barnes: What time did the evening end?

Bold-Jepson: About one, I think.

Barnes: Did you go for another swim with Kathryn?

Bold-Jepson: No, I went to bed.

Barnes: Did you see Osborne Kilgore during the evening?

Bold-Jepson: He wandered in once or twice. Early in the evening.

Barnes: How was he dressed?

Bold-Jepson: Ossie? Let me think. Shorts and a sports shirt, I think.

Barnes: (*Long pause.*) Have you ever at any time picked wild mushrooms?

Bold-Jepson: No.

Barnes: Do you know of anyone in the group, other than Kilgore, who has picked wild mushrooms?

Bold-Jepson: (*Long pause.*) No. Not offhand.

Barnes: Your wife has admitted to me that she picks mushrooms.

Bold-Jepson: Is that so? (*Short laugh.*) Chris has many talents. This is one I was not aware of.

Barnes: (*Pause.*) The afternoon of Eads's death, Kathryn Kilgore and your wife quarreled. Mrs. Bold-Jepson left immediately, I believe. Did you leave with her?

Bold-Jepson: No. I took her downstairs and put her in a cab.

Barnes: And then returned to the gathering?

Bold-Jepson: I had some unfinished church business to take care of. Our class in filmmaking needs a tremendous amount of expensive equipment. Kathryn had agreed to put in fifteen thousand if Cather Jackson, one of our richer members, would duplicate the sum. I was talking to Cather when the scene erupted.

Barnes: I see. (*Pause.*) Did he subscribe the sum you needed?

Bold-Jepson: Yes. Tentatively.

I shut the tape recorder off. It was going to be a long job. There were so many people who might offer vital information. Anyone present at the cookout or the big gathering following Kilgore's funeral. Of the immediate group, we still had Hal and Deborah Zimmerman to talk to.

Barnes and I sat around another hour discussing the tapes and formulating new questions. He finally yawned and said it was time to call it a night.

"We'll take our tape recorders to the funeral," he said. "We may just pick up some interesting conversations."

9

Eads's funeral was held in the same Madison Avenue establishment which had housed the Kilgore rites. The chapel was not quite as large, but was well filled.

It was a smaller-scale rerun of the Kilgore funeral. Susan Eads cried. Bold-Jepson conducted the service, and praised Upton in very general terms. Interment was to be private, at a later date. We were invited to Susan Eads's for a drink following the funeral.

I suspect we were only invited because I went up to speak to Bold-Jepson as he prepared to leave. Susan broke away from friends offering consolation and came over to urge him to join them. Out of politeness she included Barnes and me. Bold-Jepson hesitated, mentioning the pressures of church appointments, but agreed to stop by briefly.

In the cab Barnes said, "You say she lets these tarantulas run around loose?"

"They are harmless. Apparently."

We rode along for a while in silence. Then Barnes said, "I think I'll just drop you off there and go and see how Miller is coming along with the tape evaluations. There's no point in our both covering this thing."

"With so many people around, she'll probably have them put away safe in their big glass case. She wouldn't want someone to step on one accidentally."

He turned to look at me. "Are you implying that I'm

afraid of a few harmless tarantulas?" He grinned. "If you are, you're absolutely right."

The cab hit one of New York's better potholes and we bounced ceilingward. "Don't worry. William is a friendly little chap. He was crawling up my arm to look me in the eye and say 'hello.' "

"I have no desire to exchange greetings with any of them."

"They are ugly little monsters."

"She probably keeps them around for shock value. Eccentricity is part of the game."

"What game?"

"The game of being an artist."

"Oh." I hadn't thought of that. I had thought Susan Eads had a serious problem. Her image improved.

During my previous visit I had encountered no servants, though the immaculate condition of the place had suggested that she must have had some. Among the earliest arrivals, we were ushered in by an elderly maid who guided us to the huge living-room area and indicated the bar to us with a nod of silent disapproval.

I crossed the room to the glass case to check that both William and Tabitha were safe from harm. Tabitha, twice as big and twice as ugly as William, stood flexing her hairy legs and regarding the guests with serene detachment. William was nowhere to be seen. He may have been asleep behind one of the rocks dotting the miniature desert.

Barnes came up behind me.

"That's Tabitha. William, her son, seems to be missing."

"Permanently, I hope," said Barnes, glancing at Tabitha with distaste. "I'm going to have a drink."

There were only nine or ten guests present so far, and I didn't know any of them, though I thought I recognized Cartwright Tremd, the author. He was standing alone, near the bar, with a drink in his hand. He was a tall, angular New England type with a squint.

I approached him. "Aren't you Cartwright Tremd?"

"Yes I am," he said quickly, running the words together.

"I saw *Chastity O'Toole*. Great picture."

"It stank." He said it without emotion, still running the words together.

"I guess your book was better."

"Yes it was."

"You didn't like the picture?" What he hated was only getting five thousand for the rights. And who could blame him?

"No I didn't."

"Upton Eads was your agent, I believe."

"Yes he was."

"I hear he was one of the best."

"Bull. Lousy agent. Couldn't stand the sight of him." He continued to speak quickly, in neutral, passionless tones. "Came today out of respect for Susan."

I ordered a Scotch and then turned back to him. "I hear you only got five thousand dollars for the motion picture-rights. That's a shame."

He squinted at me more closely. "Yes it is."

"Do you blame Upton?"

The bartender handed me my drink.

"Yes I do. Bad advice."

"He advised you to take it?"

"Should have fought with me not to take it."

"Oh."

"Told me offer was pitiful but probably the only motion-picture offer I would get. Book out almost three years. Only modest sales."

I sipped my drink. "I guess it's hard to tell with these things."

"Yes it is." He finished off his own drink. "Hasn't been a total loss. New paperback sales. Big success. Make it easier to negotiate a decent sale for my next book."

I reached in my pocket and flicked off the tape recorder. So much for Kathryn's finger of suspicion. Not that I had taken it seriously anyway.

"I'll have to read the book," I said, moving down the bar.

"You do that. Buy the hardcover. Still some around. Easier to read in the hardcover. Larger type."

I looked around for Barnes. He was in a corner talking to Shunk, who had arrived unnoticed by me. I started to go over, then decided against it. Why stir up the Shunk?

Other arrivals were slowly filling the big room without walls. Kathryn, Bold-Jepson, Bentinck, Hal and Debbie Zimmerman, and Barbara Bold were in a group talking quietly. Susan, quite composed, was moving slowly among the guests accepting sympathy. Only Chris was missing. She had been at the funeral.

I strolled over and edged into the periphery of the Bold House group, flipping on the tape recorder.

"Ah, the man from Wickersham," said Bentinck.

I nodded. "Did they get your elevator repairman loose?" I asked Barbara Bold.

She smiled. "Finally. He was furious. It took four hours."

Bentinck sighed. "We'll be paying well for his fury. And the four hours."

"Barb should have negotiated the repair bill with him while he was stuck," said Hal Zimmerman.

Barbara turned to him. "Right. I should have said, "We're leaving for California shortly. Shall I call your company now, or when we get back?' "

A newcomer paused in passing and shook hands with Bentinck. Bentinck glanced at the group. "I think you know all these people. This is Larry Howe. Larry, Fergus Pringle."

I shook hands with a steely grip. For a few seconds I didn't place the name, then remembered he was the editor Kilgore had hired to handle his manuscript. I had pictured a mousy type with rimless glasses and a nervous cough. Fergus Pringle might be flabby intellectually, but physically he was pure concrete. He was about thirty-five, with wide shoulders and a slim, muscular build. He had mod, almost-shoulder-length hair and a jutting chin.

He said, "How do you do," exchanged brief pleasantries with the others, and then turned back to Bentinck. "We

95

should get together for a few minutes on Ossie's manuscript. I've given it a quick read and have a general idea of what I want to do."

Bentinck nodded. "The key word is 'cut.' Cut, cut, cut, cut."

"Well, yes, one usually has to cut."

"Of the thousand pages, you're going to have to cut at least six hundred."

"Six hundred!" Pringle's face crinkled in mock dismay. "It's not *that* bad. You've got a big book here. A fat treasure you can sell for ten ninety-five."

"I prefer a good book I can sell for seven ninety-five."

Pringle scratched his big chin. "I don't understand your reasoning. This is Kilgore's last book. Whether the critics like it or not, you're going to get a tremendous sale. Make the most of it, man."

Bentinck stared at him with stony contempt. "Bold House's reputation is a little more important to me than making a few extra dollars on Ossie's book."

Kathryn, who had been listening with interest, said, "Now just a minute. More is involved than 'a few extra dollars.' "

He shifted his eyes to her, annoyed. "What more is involved, Kathryn?"

"Ossie wanted this book published pretty much as is. He was sick of Hal cutting his books to ribbons. Since he is dead, I think we should give some consideration to his wishes."

Kathryn was giving some consideration to the higher royalties too. She hadn't even scattered poor Ossie's ashes over the North Pole yet.

"It is axiomatic that one half to two thirds of anything Ossie wrote was nauseating tripe," said Bentinck through his teeth. "I am not in business to publish nauseating tripe."

Kathryn smiled sweetly. "You don't really *have* to publish it."

Pringle broke in, "Well, I'm not going to cut six hundred pages. I'm only being paid five hundred for the job, and that doesn't cover that kind of blood, sweat, and tears."

Bentinck shrugged. "Do what you will. I suppose Hal will have to work it over and do the cutting."

Zimmerman groaned audibly.

Kathryn said, "The book will be published exactly as it comes* from Fergus. Ossie will have his whole book published, just as he wanted."

Bentinck flushed. "You keep out of this, you silly bitch. You know about as much about editing and publishing as I know about higher mathematics."

"Ben!" Barbara tugged at his arm.

Pringle said, "Just watch your language. I think you'd just better apologize to Kathryn."

Bentinck turned to give Pringle his full attention. "Indeed. And are you planning to make me?"

Pringle reached out with one big hand and grabbed a fistful of Bentinck's shirt. "I said apologize. I'm not standing by while you call Kathryn a silly bitch."

Bentinck's fist came back about seven inches, then sped forward into Pringle's midsection like a rocket. His left fist followed in a split second, delivering another rocket to Pringle's stomach.

Pringle doubled up quietly and sat on the floor, unable to get his breath. After straining and gasping for a few seconds he found it. He filled his lungs a couple of times, got shakily to his feet, and walked away.

Hardly anyone had noticed. One guest standing nearby came over.

"What happened?"

"Fell down," said Hal Zimmerman. "Stoned, I guess."

The guest nodded and went back to his own group.

"You are a crude animal," said Kathryn.

"Was that necessary, Ben?" asked Bold-Jepson.

He looked at Bold-Jepson grimly. "Try grabbing my shirtfront and threatening me, and you'll find out."

Bold-Jepson held up one hand. "Peace."

Kathryn said, "You're not going to publish Ossie's book. I'll see to that."

"We have an iron-clad contract," said Zimmerman.

"You have a three-book contract. There'll be no third book. It has to be renegotiated," said Kathryn.

Zimmerman smiled. "There is a clause that takes care of that situation. It gives Bold House the right to cop out, but not the author or his heirs."

"My lawyers say differently."

"I suspect our lawyers know more about publishing than your lawyers," said Zimmerman. "Anyway, we can let them worry about it."

"I shouldn't have called you a silly bitch," said Bentinck. "What I meant was, you're a malicious bitch."

Kathryn tossed her head and screwed up her small mouth. "Thank you. And you're a filthy animal. I'm glad there is no need for us to have any further association. And furthermore, I'm going to see that you don't get Ossie's book. Even if I have to burn the manuscript."

Lips curled back over his big white teeth, Bentinck said, "Burn away. We have a copy. And it will be edited according to Bold House standards."

"I'll sue."

"Good. I'll tie you up in litigation so long the public will forget there was ever a third-rate writer named Osborne Kilgore. Or the fifth-rate lay who married him."

She took a step toward Bentinck menacingly. "Ha, ha, then you'll never get to publish the book!"

Bentinck's nostrils wrinkled as though encountering a bad odor. "I couldn't care less. It will be a pleasure, as long as you don't make any money out of it."

"Hey," said Hal, "let's not go overboard."

He turned to Zimmerman. "I'm quite serious. Miss Hot Pants here is wrecking Bold House. Because of her, Chris is leaving. And you know how much I depend on Chris. For two cents I'd close the damned place up."

Bold-Jepson, who had been looking on with consternation, lowered his eyes. He shrugged, turned, and walked over to the bar. Kathryn gave Bentinck a long, malevolent stare, then started after Bold-Jepson, her rear end wagging in what was almost a burlesque of a sexy walk.

Barbara Bold sighed. "Well, I think we've done our bit for dear Upton's memory. Shall we leave?"

Zimmerman took his wife's arm. "Come on and buy me a free drink. I haven't seen so much excitement since the last funeral. Maybe there'll even be another murder."

"Hal! That's an awful thing to say," said Debbie.

I wandered toward the small bar with them. Barnes was standing at one end, alone. If Shunk was around, I couldn't see him.

Hal and Debbie Zimmerman headed for Barnes's end of the bar too; Kathryn and Bold-Jepson were at the other end.

"Shunk have anything new?" I asked.

Barnes eyed Hal and Debbie, who were too close for confidential reports. "I'm about ready to pack it up," he said. "I don't think this party is going to provide us with any useful information."

I mentally reviewed the scene I had just witnessed. A lot of sound and fury, but no spectacular revelations. One thing was certain. Bentinck and Kathryn were suffering from raw-edged nerves. Both had exhibited an unusual loss of control. Bentinck was more deeply upset about Chris's situation than I had realized.

"You missed a lot of excitement," I said to Barnes in a low voice.

"Oh?"

"Didn't you see Bentinck knock the corn cakes out of Fergus Pringle?"

"No." He raised his eyebrows. "Why?"

"It's all on tape. I hope."

Debbie and Hal Zimmerman moved closer. "Hey, you two," said Hal, smiling, "when are we going to get our five million bucks?"

Barnes smiled. "That's a good question."

"Ben has promised to take the whole staff to Paris for a week. We deserve it."

"I'm sure you do," said Barnes.

"Hal is getting delusions of being a rich man," said Debbie.

"Why not? My five-percent equity in Bold House has increased in value by two hundred and fifty thousand dollars," said Zimmerman.

"If Bold House ever gets it," said Debbie.

"Don't worry. We'll get it."

I signaled to the bartender and ordered a Scotch. Glancing down at the bar, I noticed an unfinished drink which had not been cleared away. Some of the liquid had spilled, and William was standing there behind the glass, tilting low in the middle to slurp it up with his ugly front end. At least I think that was what he was doing. Maybe it was his rear end, and he was sitting in it to cool off.

I moved back from the bar a bit hastily.

About that time the bartender came along with my drink. He took one look at William and did a back jump which would have qualified him for the Olympic team in the back high jump. I'm not sure they have one. Eight bottles on the rear shelves crashed to the floor.

"What the hell's going on?" yelled Zimmerman.

Lurching against the back shelves, the bartender finally recovered his balance. He looked around frantically, then grabbed a dogeared copy of the *Daily News* and advanced on William.

"Don't push him over here," yelled Barnes. The bartender was trying to sweep William off on Barnes's side of the bar.

William climbed onto the paper, which caused the bartender to drop it quickly.

Barnes picked it up, grabbing the end away from William, and shook him off onto the bar. Using the newspaper, he swept William toward the bartender's side.

"Cut that out!" yelled the bartender. He reached under the bar and came up with a sawed-off baseball bat. "You push that thing behind my bar and I swear to God I'm going to split your skull." He lifted the bat and drew back, aiming for Barnes. Barnes ducked.

Zimmerman grabbed the bartender's arm. "Cool it, buster. Put that damned thing down!"

William, who was getting pretty annoyed, flexed his hairy legs and executed a neat little jump, which put him right on Debbie Zimmerman's bare shoulder. She took one look and collapsed into Barnes's arms. This brought Barnes and William into an eye-to-eye confrontation.

I will admit Barnes has courage. He held on to Debbie and stared William down. His eyes were a little glazed, though.

Zimmerman stopped struggling with the bartender and reached hurriedly for the *Daily News*. He flicked William off Debbie's shoulder. William landed on a stool, then took a long hop to the floor.

"Don't stomp," I yelled, "he's a pet."

10

"I've got a lousy sore throat," said Miller. He sneezed wetly. "I think I'm coming down with a cold or flu. Better keep your distance."

He needn't worry, I thought. If he kept talking about it, Barnes wouldn't even stay in the same room with him.

Barnes moved a good six feet away, looking apprehensive.

Irwin Miller is a chunky ex-cop, and has developed a melon of a bay window since leaving the force. He's in the same business we're in, but we don't compete. Heading an agency specializing in security guards, Miller works mainly in the area of curbing employee pilferage and customer shoplifting. Barnes and he have a friendly working arrangement. Barnes recommends Miller for assignments of this type, and Miller recommends Barnes when the problem involves Barnes's specialties, such as insurance fraud.

Miller is a top polygraph expert. Barnes hates lie detectors. Especially when they are used in "employee relations." He considers this practice a monstrous invasion of privacy. Miller thinks he's soft-headed on the subject. They remain good friends, avoiding discussion of the topic.

Barnes regretfully concedes the value of the polygraph in crime solving. In this instance, he was almost enthusiastic about lie detection, he was so anxious to have the analysis from the new Dektor PSE equipment. I was afraid he might be relying too heavily on this ploy. Whatever we found wasn't going to be evidence. The police couldn't use it to arrest anyone, or bring him or her to trial.

Miller blew his nose. "Honest to God, Berk, I thought I had taught you how to carry out a good polygraph examination. These tapes are the toughest I've ever worked on."

Barnes stepped back another foot, as Miller had moved a few inches closer. "These people aren't strapped in your damned electric chair, you know. We can't carry on the kind of structured, official cross examination you use on some poor sniveling wretch suspected of stealing carbon paper."

Miller coughed, turning his head. "Don't knock it. Those sniveling wretches steal billions of dollars of property every year."

Barnes found a chair and sat down, managing in the process to add another couple of feet between himself and the flu. "What, specifically, is wrong with our tapes?"

Miller reached for his handkerchief again and Barnes flinched. "Mainly you got these people too goddamned excited. Remember, I warned you? Words like 'poison' and 'kill' cause stress even in innocent people. This is very sensitive equipment." He blew his nose loudly. "You've got to keep the subject very calm. Say, 'Did you do away with Mr. X?' not 'Did you poison Mr. X'?"

Barnes sighed. "It's difficult. In casual questioning, phrases such as 'Did you do away with' do not sound natural."

"Natural or not, you've got to keep the subject calm. I don't care how you phrase it, you can't go jolting the subject with words like 'poison.' "

Miller tucked his handkerchief away tidily. "Come on in the conference room and I'll show you what I mean."

The table was littered with long strips of graph paper. He selected one and handed it to Barnes, who was holding his breath, I believe.

"Take this for a for-instance. You were questioning Kathryn Kilgore."

"Larry was questioning Kathryn Kilgore."

"Larry, Schmarry, you're both lousy."

Barnes moved away. "Let's get on with it."

"Okay. Larry says, 'We are working on the theory that your husband may have been murdered.' " He pointed to the graph. "You see that mountain of stress showing up in her reply, 'Anything to delay paying up, is that it?' She's reacting to the word 'murdered.' "

"How do you know she's not reacting to the idea of not getting her five million bucks?" I asked.

He grinned. "Okay, take the next exchange. You ask, 'How would you explain Upton Eads's murder?' Look at the stress mountain when she replies, 'He was an agent, wasn't he?' Here again the word 'murder' is causing stress, and you haven't even asked her whether she did it."

Barnes laughed. "How should he have phrased it? 'We believe your husband ingested some inedible mushrooms given to him surreptitiously by some person bent upon harming him?' "

Miller smiled. "Now you're talking polygraph language."

Barnes sat down, reaching for his own handkerchief. A sympathetic sneeze was building up. "Are you saying our tapes are pretty much of a washout?"

Miller rubbed his chin thoughtfully, then picked up another graph strip. "When you have so much stress running through the whole interview, it makes it difficult to give a positive analysis. We need a calm area of nonstress so that when we hit a lie, and the bloop goes way up, we can say with confidence, 'The only reason for stress here is a lie.' " He shuffled some graph strips. "No, I wouldn't say these are a total loss. They point to certain areas you can reexplore in a calmer vein. Also, I believe you can safely eliminate certain people as suspects, though all of them seem to know more than they're willing to admit."

Barnes perked up. "Who can we eliminate?"

Miller shuffled some more graphs. "Well, let's start with Barbara Bold. She reacted strongly to the word 'murder' a couple of times, but I put that down to word reaction. I would guess that she's lying when she says it's not true that

Chris is leaving the firm. But here's the goody. When Larry asks, 'Do you suspect anyone other than Kilgore of picking the poisonous mushrooms?' you can see this mountain of stress when she says 'No.' Now look." He held the paper up for Barnes. "She doesn't react to 'Do you know definitely who picked these mushrooms?' or to 'Did you ever pick any mushrooms'? 'No' in both instances is normal. We can ask, is she reacting to the word 'poisonous' in the first question? In this case I think not. The 'poison' association is still strong in the second and third questions, even though the word itself is not used."

Barnes said, "In other words, she definitely suspects someone."

"Right."

"How does she react to the same three questions regarding Eads?"

"Equally mild stress on all three answers, probably due to the fact that the word 'poison' was used all three times."

Barnes sneezed, his handkerchief at the ready.

"Take Susan Eads, for instance. The only real stress she shows is when she claims she and Ossie were not lovers. However, it's hard to say whether it applies to the whole statement, or merely the lie about their being lovers. 'Well, we weren't,' big bloop, then smaller stress for 'Ossie wanted to divorce Kathryn and marry me. I couldn't do that to Upton.' "

I gave Barnes a couple of pills. "Cold capsules."

"I need flu capsules. Maybe I should get a shot?"

Miller said, "One thing you've confirmed here. When Larry asks, 'Upton mentioned nothing to you? About his suspicions, or what he saw?,' there is definitely no stress on her 'No.' "

Barnes sneezed again. "That's helpful, I suppose." He blew his nose. "Who else can you help us eliminate?" He chewed up the cold capsules, making me wince.

Miller dug out another set of graph strips. "Bold-Jepson, I would say. There was strong stress indicated when you suggested that Kathryn might have killed her husband to marry Bold-Jepson and still keep Kilgore's money. There was no panic when you suggested that Bold-Jepson might have done the dirty deed."

"Wonder if he has any solid reason to suspect Kathryn." I asked.

Miller nodded. "You might try to bring that out, when you question him again."

Barnes's head was drooping. "I think I'll go home and go to bed," he said. "Larry, you stay and make detailed notes. We'll go over this in the morning."

I was expendable. Let me get the flu. I followed him to the door. "This is all psychosomatic, you know. If you were catching something from Miller, you wouldn't be showing symptoms this soon. It would be—"

"How long?"

"I don't know. Maybe a week. Certainly not in fifteen minutes."

"You see, you don't *know.*"

I shook my head and went back to Miller.

Miller looked at his watch. "No point in hanging around here all night," he said. "I'll give you a ten-minute course on how to read Dektor graphs, then you can take the whole damned shooting match home with you and study it at your leisure."

Typical, I thought. Nobody works but Larry.

Once you got the hang of it, the graphs were simple enough to read. They were presented so that the markings would be similar to those produced by a polygraph stylus. Many technicians were using both systems, one to confirm the other, and it was handier to have the markings similar. Stress on the Dektor graph was actually indicated by blocking of the voice waveform produced by the absence of the normal inaudible FM vibrations. The actual words spoken were presented on typewritten strips pasted below the graph markings.

We stuffed the strips in big envelopes, one for each tape, and I shook hands with Miller, wishing him good night and a happy flu.

"I think I've definitely got a temperature," he said.

I found a cab and got to my apartment with only about ten minutes of traffic jam. I called Isabel and suggested that she might want to come over and help me study graphs.

"I've never heard it called that before," she said, "but I guess I might as well."

I ordered a pizza from my nearby unfriendly pizzeria (we deliver, but not without an argument), fetched a half gallon of red wine from the cupboard under the sink, cleaned off the kitchen table, and sat down to work.

Kathryn's tape was a confusing mess. I could see why Miller had been discouraged. There were so many stress signals that nothing stood out. "Murder" brought it on, "poisoned" caused mountains everywhere, even when she said, "Poisoned. What a horrible word. No one tells me anything."

I dug out some four-by-six cards and made notes. Kathryn's score came out as follows:

Wherever the word "murder" or "poison" was used, medium to high stress.

"You told me you didn't know anything about wild mushrooms." Answer, "I don't." Medium stress.

"You say you've never picked mushrooms." Answer, "Certainly not." Medium stress.

The whole conversation about mushrooms. Medium to high stress.

"I've heard rumors that Ossie wanted to divorce you, etc." Answer, medium to high stress.

"Whoever put Amanita in with the other mushrooms must be a monster. She or he could have killed a dozen people." Answer, "No one did, etc." Medium to high stress.

"Your attitude is insulting, etc." High stress.

"I don't have to talk to you." High stress.

"I don't care whether your crummy insurance company pays the money or not, etc." High stress.

"Please leave. This conversation is ended." High stress.

Obviously my questions had excited Kathryn so much she continually lost her FM vibrations. Putting it that way, it sounded sort of sexy.

The end of the tape was strange. I had asked, "Will you please state unequivocally, yes or no, did you put poisoned mushrooms in your husband's concoction?" Her answer, "No," dropped down to below normal in stress.

11

Isabel arrived with the pizza, which was good timing. The guy who delivers was so busy ogling her nifty shape he didn't get a chance to sneer much at my fifty-cent tip. Why these guys expect folding bread for a one-pizza, four-block delivery, I can't figure.

Isabel followed me into the kitchen, eyeing the pile of graph strips on the table. "You really did want to study graphs," she said, astonished.

I pushed the strips aside and made room for the pizza. "Why not? You have any better ideas?"

She reached to open the pizza. "No. Of course not. No, certainly not."

I poured us both glasses of wine. "You can study me if the graphs get boring."

"Study you gobbling pizza?"

This was a snide reference to the fact that when we share a pizza it's an unwritten rule that I get two thirds of it. My 175 pounds require more sustenance than her 115. Of course, if she wanted more than a third, I would insist upon her having it, even if we had to buy two pizzas.

I cut a slab and handed it to her. "I want you to cast all the women's lib propaganda out of your mind, and put your feminine intuition to work on some graphs."

Using a folded napkin as a holder for one corner, she took a dainty bite. "Oh, we admit that women are more intuitive than men."

In between munching and quaffing I explained the Dektor graph markings and told her how we goofed by stirring up too much excitement. When we finished and cleared the debris away I gave her the set prepared from Kathryn's tape.

"Here's your chance to be intuitive about a real bitchy character. Look these over and tell me what you think."

She took them and glanced at the top strip. "She's guilty as hell," she said.

"You're not that intuitive. Read them."

I opened the envelope containing Bentinck Bold's graphs and settled down to work.

It was satisfying to note that Barnes had blown his interview with Bentinck fully as badly as I had mine with Kathryn. Excitement bloomed all over the graph tapes. Starting with, "Would you mind describing your movements the evening Kilgore died?" there was stress everywhere, even on such innocuous statements as "Barbara and I strolled down to the beach and watched the waves crash in for a while," "We were kicking around possible titles," and "The others were inside playing bridge or watching television. Or whatever."

Even Kilgore's clothes caused stress. After the question, "How was Kilgore dressed?" the answer, "Dressed? I'm not sure I remember. Let me see. Shorts, moccasins, sport shirt? I think," caused a sizable bloop. The answer "Yes" to the question, "He had just completed a manuscript?" caused a mountain. How could you evalute anything when statements of known facts caused stress?

Wild mushrooms, aconite, Eads's death, Bentinck's digestion being better when he took a walk after meals, meeting Upton Eads in the woods, Kilgore's possible divorce action against Kathryn, Kilgore's persecution of Bold-Jepson, the possibility of Christiana leaving Bold House, and practically everything else caused mountainous country. Understandably, subjects such as Chris leaving Bold House were upsetting. These were nervous, highly sensitive people. Apparently everything associated with the two deaths also caused stress.

I noted all the stress areas on my cards, which seemed pretty useless, but at least I was being methodical. Barnes was getting his money's worth tonight.

"This is absolutely fascinating," said Isabel. "I think I'll take it up as a hobby."

"What's the verdict?"

"I still say she's guilty."

"Why?"

"Intuition."

I stuffed Kathryn's graph tapes back in the envelope and poured us both more wine. "Your intuition needs to go in the shop for a new carburetor. Didn't you notice the last question I asked her? 'Yes or no, did you put poison mushrooms in your husband's concoction?' When she answered 'No,' her temperature was subnormal. She was telling the truth."

She sipped her wine and gave me her idea of a dark, mysterious look. "Just you wait, you'll see."

I handed her the Bentinck Bold graph tapes, then opened Christiana's envelope.

Isabel placed her hand palm down on the Bentinck tapes and stared into space. "He's guilty," she said.

"Oh come on, now you're using ESP. That isn't even as reliable as intuition."

"I'm getting very bad vibes."

I pulled out Christiana's tapes. "Read the damned things. Study the graphs. ESP we can't use."

Christiana's tapes were almost as bad as Bentinck's. She was either lying or emotionally upset about picking wild mushrooms, about when she picked them last, about Eads being killed, about Kathryn having an affair with her husband, about playing tennis with Bentinck, about having breakfast, about everything. This girl was a nervous wreck. I laboriously made notes for Barnes.

I poured more wine and waited for Isabel to finish studying Bentinck's graphs.

"Well?"

"Guilty as charged."

"Oh hell, they both can't be guilty. One thing I couldn't accept, those two cooperating to murder Kilgore."

"Guilty, guilty, guilty."

I gave her Christiana's graphs. She rested her hand on them and went through her act, staring into space and batting her eyelashes.

"This one is clean. My vibes are troubled, but not bad. These are woeful vibes."

I drank some wine. "Maybe she killed them both sadly."

"With affectionate reluctance."

"Yeah."

She blinked at me sadly.

"Cut out the witch stuff and read them."

"Okay."

I went into the ten-by-twelve box the management larcenously calls a living room and collapsed on the sofa. In a few seconds I was dozing. I dreamed Isabel was a witch kneeling naked before a small fire sputtering noxious vapors.

"I'm leaving," said Isabel, waking me.

I sat up. "Hey, don't go. We have a lot to talk about."

"It's late."

"You'd better sleep over, or I'll have to escort you."

"No."

"Why not?"

"You take me too much for granted."

I could never figure out why girls worry so much about being taken too much for granted.

"I love you. Sit down and tell me what you thought of Christiana's tape."

She sat down next to me. "You know, it's really scary. I got those woeful vibes without even knowing anything about Christiana."

"I know. It jolted me."

"I wouldn't want to start seeing into the future, and things like that."

I took her in my arms and kissed her. "If you're going to be a witch, we could use you in the business."

12

Barnes had recovered from his pseudo flu, but was in a nasty humor instead. He grumbled his way through my painfully compiled notes, then studied the graph tapes for some time, muttering and sighing at frequent intervals.

Finally he said, "We're going to change our strategy."

A commander facing defeat may have to change his strategy to save the day.

"Instead of working alone, I think we'll do better visiting these people together. We'll structure our questioning on the Mutt and Jeff routine. But with a different objective, of course. The good guy will keep everything calm and friendly, and will do most of the talking. The bad guy will ask cautiously worded key questions from time to time."

I said, "With plenty of intervals between each of the key questions to keep the seas very calm."

"Right."

I thought about it for a few seconds. It might work very well. Though in Kathryn's case, it was hard to visualize getting warm and friendly with her.

"Sounds okay. I'll be the good guy. I have a lot of natural charisma."

Barnes laughed, which is pretty rare for him. "Charm you may have, but I'm afraid I'm going to have to be the good guy and do the buttering up. Coming from a youngster this kind of thing frequently rubs the wrong way. These are shrewd, sophisticated people." He consulted his cigarette notebook, then scribbled the time, place, and number of the treat he was preparing to light. "The reaction can be, 'Who does this squirt think he's conning?' "

"If I can't be the good guy, I'm going over and play with the kids in the next block."

Barnes lit his cigarette, still in a good humor. "While you're there, see if one of the kids wants a good job."

We spent the next hour preparing the key questions I would ask. Barnes was certain he could ad-lib his role of warm, friendly confidant.

Since we hadn't officially interviewed Hal and Debbie Zimmerman, Barnes decided to get these two chores out of the way before staging our repeat performances with the stars of our suspect list.

Hal Zimmerman's office was cluttered and comfortable, with book-lined walls and manuscripts stacked everywhere. He was preoccupied when he stepped around his desk to shake hands. He went back to his chair and sat down while we stood wondering where to sit. All the chairs had manuscripts on them.

"Sit anywhere," said Zimmerman. "Just put the stuff on the floor."

We carefully transferred manuscripts to the floor, which was nicely carpeted in red and gold tweed, and sat down.

"When are we going to get our five million dollars?" asked Zimmerman, grinning.

Barnes flashed him a big, genial smile. "Soon, no doubt, soon."

Zimmerman perked up. "That's good news."

Barnes nodded. "Probably just about double the value of your Bold House stock, I would imagine."

"At least." He hesitated. "Well, perhaps not. It's hard to assess the value of a publishing company until you get down to looking for a buyer. And we never have."

"Anyway, it will be quite a bonanza."

"That it will."

"I'm pleased that we'll be able to make everybody so happy. An all-expense trip to Europe and all that," said Barnes.

"Could I ask you a question, Hal," I interrupted. "Do you suspect anyone of picking those harmful mushrooms, other than Kilgore?"

They both looked at me as though I had belched rudely.

"No, I do not suspect anyone," said Zimmerman.

Barnes yawned, probably faking it. "Looks like it's going to be another beautiful day. Warm and sunny, but not too hot."

"We can use it," said Zimmerman, relaxing.

"As soon as we wrap this case up, I'm going to take a vacation," said Barnes. "Maybe Mexico or Spain."

They chatted for a few minutes about places to go in Mexico and Spain.

"Hal," I asked, "do you know definitely of anyone picking harmful mushrooms?"

He turned to me with a hard little smile. "I started to say that you're asking an asinine question. But I see your distinction. If I *knew*, I wouldn't suspect. The answer is no, I don't know of anyone who picked harmful mushrooms."

Barnes looked at me, magnificently bored. "Have you ever been in Hong Kong, Hal? I've always wanted to go there."

He turned back to Barnes. "As a matter of fact, yes." He described a trip he had made to Hong Kong to negotiate with an author. The story was long enough, I thought, to induce sufficient calm.

"Did you ever pick any harmful mushrooms?" I asked.

He looked at me, annoyed. "No."

"For heaven's sake, Larry. Leave this nonsense to Lieutenant Shunk. Hal is not a suspect."

Zimmerman looked at him sharply. "If I'm not a suspect, why are you here?"

Barnes sighed. "Just touching all the bases. Speaking of bases—"

They talked for five minutes about baseball.

115

"Hal, do you suspect anyone of administering aconite to Upton Eads?" I asked when there was a lull in the assessment of the Mets' chances.

Zimmerman fingered his goatee thoughtfully. "No, I do not suspect anyone. Nor do I know *definitely* who slipped it to him. And lastly, I personally did not poison Upton Eads."

Pretty sharp. He had learned our formula in one lesson.

Barnes sighed deeply and gave me a pitying look. "This boy can't give up. He's got to play detective night and day."

This was the end of part one, the structured half of our interview. Since roaming freely over the subject created too much stress, we decided to begin by presenting a sylvan lake of calm. We would splash it from time to time with only a few upsetting pebbles. This part of the tape could be set aside for Dektor analysis. During the rest of the questioning we could stir up as much trouble as we wanted to. If there was any useful information lying around, we might pick it up easier this way than we could pussy-catting with beautiful weather and trips to Mexico.

"Hal, we know someone murdered Eads, and we're damned sure someone murdered Kilgore," said Barnes. "Do you think Kathryn Kilgore would be capable of putting poison mushrooms in her husband's stew?"

Zimmerman thought for a few seconds. "Yes, I think she would be *capable* of it. I won't say that I think she did it."

"Tell us what you did the morning of the cookout, and that evening."

Barnes's tone had become so businesslike that even Zimmerman could sense the falling away of the good guy. He looked puzzled.

"In the morning? I woke up late, had breakfast on the terrace with Debbie. Chris joined us. After breakfast, I went back to our room and worked until lunch. During the evening? There was dinner, then Debbie and I played Gin. Went to bed."

"Did you see Kilgore during the morning, or after dinner?"

"During the morning, no. I vaguely remember seeing him

after dinner. He wasn't playing bridge, but I think he came in briefly."

"Any idea of the time?"

"No."

"When you were at the gathering following Kilgore's funeral, did you particularly notice anyone who spent time talking to Eads?"

Zimmerman thought it over. "Not really. I think I remember seeing him with Kathryn, but that would be natural. Since he was executor, they'd have plenty to discuss."

Debbie Zimmerman stuck her head in the door.

"I'm in town and you can take me to lunch."

Zimmerman stood up, obviously pleased. "Come in, dear. You're in town, but I can't take you to lunch. I'm being taken to lunch by an agent. A sexy redhead."

"I'll snatch her baldheaded," said Debbie. She had a trace of a Southern accent.

Barnes and I had also gotten up. He gestured, offering her his chair. "Have lunch with us. Not only will we be delighted, but it would be a kindness on your part. We were going all the way up to Westport to see you."

"You were coming to Westport to see *me*? Why?"

Barnes blinked. "Just making the rounds. We're trying to tie up this Kilgore investigation."

"But why me?"

"You are one of the inner circle."

She looked at her husband. "Should I go to lunch with them?"

He cocked his head. "Sure. Anything for five million dollars. Even if you have to"—he inclined his head slightly in Barnes's direction and winked—"you know."

"Hal!"

Barnes laughed, embarrassed.

"You're awful. Now I won't go." She sat down and crossed her legs. "On second thought, I will go. As long as I'm worth five million dollars."

Zimmerman said, "Not one penny less."

Baccara is one of Barnes's favorite bistros. After chatting another five minutes while Zimmerman's secretary telephoned to see whether a reservation was possible, we left and cabbed the few blocks to the restaurant.

Debbie, who seemed mildly amused at the idea of having lunch with us, said, "I can't imagine what I can contribute to your big investigation."

"You were on the scene," I said as we were being ushered to a choice table. Barnes is a favorite customer.

"So were at least fifty other people."

Barnes muttered, "This is one of our little problems." He gave the waiter our drink order. A vodka martini for Debbie, Glenlivet for us.

Barnes went through his routine, and I went through mine, throwing in my nasty little questions in the most relaxed moments. This carried us through cocktails and smoked salmon with capers. By the time the Sole Bonne Femme arrived, we had started picking her brain for what she might remember of the crucial periods.

"Unfortunately, my memory is about as far from total recall as you can get," said Debbie. "I don't even remember if I spoke to Upton Eads that day."

"You do remember seeing him, at least?" asked Barnes.

"Oh, yes. Of course. I was standing near him at one point. I remember hearing Kathryn say something to him." She pondered, attacking the fish with enthusiasm. It was *real* Dover sole. "This is absolutely delicious."

"And what did she say?" asked Barnes.

Debbie thought.

Finally she shook her head and ate some more sole.

"*Fresh*, that's what she said."

"Fresh?"

She shrugged apologetically. "That's the only word I can remember. There was something else, of course."

The waiter came to pour more Pouilly-Fuissé.

"Oh, well. Probably not important," said Barnes. "Do you recall seeing Kilgore at any time after dinner? The evening he died?"

She sipped her replenished glass of wine. "Sure. He came in the room while Hal and I were playing Gin."

"Did he seem ill?"

"Not that I noticed."

"Did you talk to him?"

She thought for a few seconds. "We may have kidded a bit. I don't remember."

"Do you remember what he was wearing?"

She shook her head. "I was having so much fun beating Hal, I wasn't paying much attention to Ossie." She put her fork down, sighing, then perked up. "Wait a minute. I remember. He was wearing navy blue shorts and a red checked sport shirt."

"Navy blue shorts? Are you sure?"

She nodded. "Positive. I remember thinking they were so conservative. Ossie usually wore bright, wild colors."

We paused for the dessert order. Everyone opted for Cranshaw melon.

"Blue shorts," said Barnes after the waiter left. "That's strange."

"Why?" I asked.

He turned to me. "That's not what Kilgore left on the beach when he went for his fatal swim. At least, not according to Marino's report. 'One bath towel, large. One pair of shorts, red. One sports shirt, yellow and blue stripes. Moccasins, brown. Shorts, jockey.' "

Barnes *does* have almost total recall. I asked Debbie, "You're not color-blind?"

"I certainly am not."

Barnes rubbed his chin. "Why would he have changed clothes? What time in the evening did you see him?"

"Early. Shortly after dinner, I believe."

"Maybe he just got out of his formal dinner clothes to be more comfortable," I said.

Debbie smiled. "Don't laugh. Navy blue shorts might have been his idea of black tie. Things were very informal at Swigatchit. The only rule for dinner was that the men had to cover their hairy chests with something, shirt or sweater."

"Not being hairy, the women didn't have to?" I asked.

Debbie fumbled for a cigarette. I lit it for her. "No one tested it, but I believe going topless would have been out of order, as far as Kathryn was concerned. Though she wore see-through blouses occasionally."

The melon arrived. From Barnes's expression, he was finding the conversation unproductive.

We had trouble getting in to see Kathryn. The maid returned to the foyer and said madam would not be able to receive us. Barnes sent her back, asking her to tell madam it was urgent. The maid returned with the word that madam did not consider it urgent for her.

Barnes said, "Tell her that if she doesn't see me, I'll have to come back with Lieutenant Shunk. I think she'll see him."

Kathryn came out pouting.

"Your assistant was very rude to me."

"Sorry," I said.

"I'm sure he didn't mean to offend you," said Barnes.

"Oh yes he did."

"No, really. I didn't mean to. Never," I said.

She had gardening gloves in one hand and a trowel in the other. She turned and led us into the apartment. We followed her out to the terrace.

Barnes paused by a huge flowerbox which occupied an area at least fifteen feet long by about seven wide.

"Oh, no. It can't be," he said.

"Cannabis," said Kathryn.

"You'd better not let Shunk see this."

"These plants were imported from Yucatan. The very finest leaf."

Nothing but the best for Ossie.

"Regardless of the quality, growing marijuana is still very much against the law," said Barnes. "You could go to jail, you know."

She smiled.

"In fact, it is really my duty to report this to Shunk," said Barnes.

She gave him a knowing look. "But you won't, though, and you know it."

"Why not?"

"Because it's none of your business if Ossie wanted to grow his own pot. I'll donate them to a hospital, or something, if necessary."

We moved to one of the conversation areas and sat down.

Barnes remembered that he was the good guy. "I was just joking. Seriously, though, I'm surprised Shunk or one of the other cops didn't notice. They are trained to look for cannabis. It's very embarrassing when a big patch is discovered."

"Like a half a block from the police station," I said.

"Would they really put me in jail?"

"Quite possibly. Growing and selling it is a much more serious offense than simple possession."

She shrugged. "Oh, well, I won't invite them out on the terrace if they come again."

As the good guy, Barnes found it tough going. He tried the weather, politics, home furnishings, and got monosyllabic, disinterested replies. She evinced some interest in the theater, and during this discussion I slipped in my questions.

"Do you suspect anyone of feeding harmful mushrooms to your husband?"

"Yes. He picked them and fed them to himself."

"Do you know definitely who provided harmful mushrooms to Osborne Kilgore?"

"Yes, what is this? Ossie picked them himself."

"Come on, Larry, quit trying to be the superdetective," said Barnes. "You're beginning to sound like a broken record."

I let them chat for another five minutes, then asked, "Did you put harmful mushrooms in your husband's Mushrooms Ossie-Tabasco?"

"No, I did not."

Her mouth had tightened and she was obviously irritated. Barnes had a rough time getting her back on smooth seas so that I could ask the three questions about Eads. He managed it by bringing the subject around to fashion, drawing her out on the famous couturiers she patronized in Rome and Paris. During this discussion I managed to get my questions in, causing only momentary upsets, Barnes remonstrating with me each time.

"If I remember correctly," said Barnes, "the last time you saw your husband alive was about nine-thirty that evening. Do you remember how he was dressed?"

She squeezed a fistful of her long black hair, then patted it smooth. "Dark blue shorts and a red shirt, I think."

"These are not the clothes he left on the beach."

She raised her eyebrows.

"At that time he was wearing red shorts and a blue and yellow striped shirt."

She shook her head. "I'm sure he was wearing dark blue shorts. We were playing bridge, but I have a definite mental image of him standing there grinning."

"Why would he have changed?"

She tilted her head back and thought. "Ossie was sort of at loose ends when he finished a book. For nine or ten months he lived like a monk, researching it and writing it. Then he would take a couple of months off. All he wanted to do was eat, drink and—" She stopped, a little confused.

Barnes nodded, smiling. "But how does this relate to his changing clothes at nine-thirty or later, when he apparently wasn't planning to go anywhere or see anyone?"

She looked at him, mildly exasperated. "I'm trying to explain. When he was between books he did things like that. He bought tons of new clothes, and frequently changed for no reason at all. Maybe just because he wanted to see how they looked. The new ones, I mean."

Barnes sighed, discouraged. "Oh."

I said, "The day Upton Eads died, you were talking to him, and you were overheard saying something was *fresh*. Do you recall the incident?"

She switched her eyes to me quickly. "*Who* overheard me say that?"

"You don't recall it?"

"No. Who says I said it?"

"I don't remember. I'd have to consult my notes."

"It was Chris, wasn't it?"

I shook my head.

"Why are you lying to me?"

She stood up, agitated. "You're deliberately being evasive. You know very well who said it."

Barnes stood up. "Why are you so excited?"

"I'm not excited. I resent this kind of question. I do not wish to be toyed with."

13

We had to wait twenty-five minutes to see Bentinck Bold, and when we did get into his office we found him grim and unfriendly. The office was bigger, of course, than Zimmerman's, with more books from floor to ceiling, more chairs, more potted plants. There were no manuscripts on the chairs, though a number were stacked on his large, curved desk.

"I have a business to run, and I'm short-handed," he said. "I can't give you much time." He took out an immaculate white handkerchief and mopped his forehead. "Without Chris, things do not run very well around here."

"Your sister carried out her plan to leave?" asked Barnes.

He tucked the handkerchief away. "I don't know. One thing is certain, she hasn't been working. And there are a hundred and one things she was working on that need to be resolved."

Barnes skillfully steered the conversation into the problems of the publishing business. The spring list, not the books that were being distributed now, but next year's, was a mess. Verbal offers she had made to certain agents were unconfirmed. Contracts which were being negotiated had been left unfinished. Advertising schedules for current books had remained on her desk unapproved, resulting in newspapers and magazines closing without the ads. Orders for binding additional copies of books selling well had not been placed.

Bentinck was so absorbed in these problems that I managed to ease in my six questions with no more reaction than a few hostile stares. With these out of the way, Barnes settled himself more comfortably in his chair.

"The evening of Kilgore's death, when you were chatting with him about a title for his forthcoming book, did you notice what color shorts he was wearing? Or the color of his shirt?" Barnes asked.

Bentinck looked puzzled. "Color? I'm afraid not."

"It seems that he left different clothes on the beach than those he was wearing earlier when he was briefly with the bridge players."

"Oh?"

"Probably not important."

Bentinck shrugged. "Hal tells me you said your investigation was practically over and that we should have our check soon."

Barnes smiled. "I may have given him that impression. I sincerely hope things work out that way."

"We can certainly use the money. If Chris really wants out, it's going to put the whammy on our cash flow."

I said, "At the cookout, you advised me not to eat the Mushrooms Ossie-Tabasco."

He looked at me, eyebrows raised. "I did?"

I nodded.

"I may have. You were not one of the regulars, and Mushrooms Ossie-Tabasco have been known to spoil a guest's whole afternoon. Not fatally, however."

"I thought perhaps it was because you knew it contained Amanita phalloides."

He rubbed his bearded cheek, smiling. "You are a nasty chap, aren't you? It's the last time I play Good Samaritan."

Barnes asked, "When you were walking in the woods the morning of the cookout, did you see anyone other than Upton Eads?"

Bentinck's lips curled downward on one side. "No. I think I answered that question before."

I hesitated, entering the elevator at the Bolds' townhouse.

If we got stuck in there, Barnes would probably develop low blood sugar, galloping arthritis, or at the very least a trotting migraine. I had no medications for the first two.

We made it safely to the fourth floor. Christiana answered the door. She looked so completely miserable that I felt like saying, "Excuse me, we'll come back some other time."

She said, "You might as well come in, I suppose."

She had obviously lost weight, thinning her already slender figure. Her face was taut, and her large eyes looked even larger. And sadder. She walked slowly and cautiously ahead of us, as though following a path along a precipice.

The large living room was at the front, overlooking the street. Except for one small area, it was as neat as a model room for a furniture ad. The corner she led us to appeared to have been inhabited steadily for days. Ashtrays on the coffee table were full and spilling over. Wadded-up Kleenexes littered the carpet. A half-filled quart of Black Label Scotch stood in a sticky puddle that had missed the glass.

She poured herself a drink shakily, offering the bottle to Barnes in a silent gesture.

He shook his head. "Thanks no, not right now."

She raised her drink, looking at Barnes over the rim. "Well?"

"I have a feeling we are intruding," said Barnes.

She sipped her drink. "I would say so. Yes. On the other hand, I really have nothing better to do."

"Are you ill?"

"Ill?" She considered the question gravely. "I suppose so. I suppose being unpleasantly stoned over a period might come under that category."

"Your brother is having his problems without you."

She swirled her drink slowly, staring at the glass. "Yes, I can imagine he is. I'm sorry. I'm afraid I've"—she—paused—"lost interest in Bold House. Along with a number of other things."

Barnes eyed the bottle of Scotch. Had there been a clean glass available, I think he would have helped himself. Women who are even slightly out of control make him nervous.

"I'm sure you'd like to see the matter of the insurance claim resolved," said Barnes.

She shook a cigarette from one of the several half-empty packages on the coffee table. Barnes lit it for her.

"Yes, of course. Of course. That's really all I'm waiting around for." There was a long pause. "I can use it. I might even leave it, or give it," she amended quickly, "to some great university. I could establish the Christiana Bold Chair for Unresolved Women."

The conversation continued in this apathetic vein. We had wanted calm. We had it here. The scene was calmer than an empty viewing chamber in an undertaking establishment. My questions caused an occasional ripple of interest, but certainly no excitement.

Barnes said, "The afternoon Upton Eads died, you had a rather spectacular quarrel with Kathryn Kilgore."

"Yes."

She nodded drowsily. "That silly, stupid bitch. She was here this morning." She gulped another ounce of Scotch, then puffed furiously on her cigarette. "You wouldn't *believe* how stupid she is. She offered me her entire five-million-dollar settlement from Wickersham if I would agree to divorce Bob." She crushed the cigarette out and lit another quickly. "I told her to get a note from Bob stating that he wished to marry her, and she could have him absolutely free. I'd even throw in a book of green stamps to go with the deal."

"I gather you think Bob is not likely to marry her."

She nodded with dreamy overemphasis. "If she waits for Bob to marry her, she will be long in the tooth indeed. Yes, very long in the tooth."

I was afraid she was falling asleep, or ready to pass out. Barnes asked quickly, "The afternoon of Eads's death, did you notice Kathryn talking to him?"

"I don't remember."

"Debbie Zimmerman overheard her say something to him. Something about *fresh.*"

"Fresh?"

Christiana lifted her glass again, her hand trembling. "Of course she poisoned him. You know that, don't you?"

Her tone was so casual Barnes was momentarily jolted. He replied in the same quiet tone, "No, I didn't know. Did you see her poison him?"

"Of course. She had a little bowl. She dumped a spoonful of something on his plate. It was undoubtedly poison."

Barnes glanced at me, interest perking. "You saw her dump a spoonful of something on Eads's plate?"

"I did, yes."

"Did he know she was doing it? I mean, was it done while he was not looking?"

She lit another cigarette. Smoke was still curling up from a freshly lit one in the ashtray. "Oh, he saw her. He was grinning like a beagle waiting for his Alpo."

14

Miller was home with the flu. Kramer, his second in command, was in Detroit. None of the lower echelon present had been trained in the use of the new Dektor equipment.

I telephoned Barnes and gave him the options. One, Miller would probably be in tomorrow. Kramer would definitely be back the following day. Two, we could try to find another agency in New York that had Dektor equipment. Three, we could send or take the new tapes to Dektor's main headquarters near Washington and have them processed there.

Barnes muttered and "tsk-tsked" for a few seconds, then sneezed, remembering he had been exposed to Miller's flu. He decided to leave the tapes for Miller and hope he'd be in tomorrow. Any other arrangement would take just as long, if not longer.

"We might as well take a run up to Swigatchit. See if Marino is making any progress," he said.

I pointed out that it was a bit late in the day to start running up to Swigatchit, and that he should at least call and find out whether Marino would be on duty in the evening when we arrived.

He agreed that this was sensible.

"On your way back to the office, stop in and see Kathryn Kilgore. Ask her what she served Eads. You know, the situation Christiana described."

Sutton Place wasn't on my way back to the office. In fact, it was tiresomely and boringly out of the way. Not only that, tackling Kathryn twice in one day was one time more than I cared to tackle. However, a man must earn his bread.

She wouldn't see me.

"Tell her I left my frangeful on the terrace," I said to the maid.

She sent word back that my frangeful, or whatever it was, wasn't there.

"How does she know?"

"She looked," said the maid.

"I'll bet she doesn't even know where to look for a frangeful."

The maid backed away, a little frightened. "I don't even know what a frangeful is, and neither does madam. And madam *does not* want to see you."

"Tell her it's the filter from my hashish pipe, and I never smoke without it."

Kathryn came rushing out, her hair tousled, looking like an angry schoolgirl who has been roughed up by some bad boys.

"Just what are you trying to pull with this hashish bit?" she yelled. "Are you trying to blackmail me? I'll have you put in jail!"

The maid, a sweet-faced little Puerto Rican girl, stood watching us openmouthed.

"Barnes wanted me to ask you a couple of questions. Won't take but a minute."

She glared at me, then turned to the maid. "Teresa, you can leave us, please. I'll call you if I need you."

The maid left, switching her behind importantly.

"Christiana Bold-Jepson says you offered her five million dollars to divorce her husband."

She opened her mouth, then closed it. She half turned to leave, then said, "Maybe we should talk. Come in."

We stopped short of the terrace this trip. She paused in the huge, cathedral-ceilinged living room, then sat down carefully at one end of a big sofa, smoothing her skirt to effect a neat arrangement.

"Sit down, Larry," she said, her voice softening faster than chocolate melting in your hand. "I'd like to explain about Chris. The poor girl is sick. She's on the borderline."

I sat down facing her. "She seemed okay to me. Mentally, that is. Perfectly coherent."

She shook her head. "You just don't *know*. The poor thing is on the verge of madness. I live in mortal fear that she will be committed any day."

"Why do you live in mortal fear?"

She hestitated. "Well, what I mean. That is, if she's— Oh, hell, Bob will never be able to get a divorce."

"Does Bob want a divorce?"

She smirked shyly. "What do you think? They are dreadfully unhappy."

"Did you really offer her five million dollars?"

She leaned over and put her hand on my knee. "Do you think I would *seriously* offer her five million dollars?"

"Why not? It's only money."

She removed her hand. "I think I said she could have the whole damned settlement, if Wickersham ever paid it, which I am beginning to doubt. I said that because she said she was only waiting for her share of the Bold House claim. That she was going away, alone, when she got it. I didn't mean it, *really.*"

Her long, rapid explanation left her slightly breathless. She leaned back and looked at me.

"Of course, if Chris *wanted* some of the money I would give it to her. I had planned to give quite a bit of it to the church, and it occurred to me that the church would be far better off if Bob was divorced. Chris keeps him so upset he really doesn't function the way he should. He has so much to *give.* You can't weigh it in terms of money."

If she handed it out fifteen thousand dollars at a time, she could play lady bountiful to the Church of the Expanding Awareness for a long time.

"The day Upton Eads died, you were speaking to him and you had a small bowl in your hand. You put a spoonful of something on his plate. Do you recall the incident?"

She was staring into space absentmindedly. "No."

"You mean you didn't?"

She looked at me. "No, I just don't remember. He may have asked for mayonnaise or something."

She leaned over and touched my knee again. "Larry, I have a problem you may be able to help me with. There would be a nice fee in it for you."

"Oh?"

"There's that stupid provision in Ossie's will. His ashes have to be scattered on the North Pole. Bentinck was going to take care of it, but—"

She and Bentinck were not exactly friends any more. "I understand," I said.

"If you would take over making the arrangements, go up there and see that it's done properly, it would be such a relief to me."

"Me, go to the North Pole?"

She leaned forward again. "Think how exciting it will be to *see* the North Pole. And you'll be well paid for the trip. Say—" She bit her little finger gently. "Say five thousand dollars plus expenses?"

Five thousand dollars. I couldn't believe it. Isabel would flip. What a load of bread for our copout fund. This wasn't bread, it was a whole damned bakery.

"You'd come along for the ceremony, I suppose?"

Her eyes widened. "I'd love to, especially with *you*, Larry. Unfortunately I have this sinus condition, and the bitter cold—well, it would just be impossible. I know Ossie would understand."

When the candy-colored lights stopped flashing I decided I was being offered a bribe. Why was she trying to get me out of the picture? Didn't she know Barnes was the brains of the team? Did she think I was more of a threat because I had been playing the bad guy, and had asked the embarrassing questions?

132

On the other hand, the five thousand was tempting. Maybe it wasn't a bribe. She had to comply with the provisions of the will, and perhaps five thousand didn't seem the gross overpayment to her that it seemed to me. It would certainly take some doing. I had no idea of what was involved. Find an Eskimo village with a bushwhacking pilot willing to make the trip? How did I get to the Eskimo village? And even after I got there, I might have to wait for several days for the weather to be right. Then, of course, would Barnes give me a short leave of absence to do the job?

"It would certainly be interesting," I said. "I've always wanted to go to the North Pole. But I'll have to think about it. There are various problems."

"What problems?"

"Well, for one thing, I might lose my job. I'll have to weigh the five thousand against the possibility of losing a good job."

She nibbled her little finger some more. "Oh, pooh. I'm sure Mr. Barnes would let you take a few days off."

I hailed a cab and inched my way over to the Canadian government offices on Fifth Avenue.

"I want to go to the North Pole," I said. "I mean, actually go to it, not fly over it in a 747 eight miles up."

The clerk, sober-faced and middle-aged, had a high forehead and wore thick-rimmed plastic framed glasses. He looked me over carefully, then reached for some schedules.

"Let me see." He flipped through them. "The earliest Nordair flight you could get from Montreal would be at eleven-fifteen tomorrow morning, arriving at Resolute Bay at sixteen-twenty. There are several Air Canada flights to Montreal that would get you there in time for the Nordair flight. Once you get to Resolute Bay, you can contact Sam MacIntosh, of MacIntosh Aviation. He'll fly you to the Pole."

I stared at him. I think my mouth may have been hanging open. "It's that easy?"

He smiled. "Well—"

"I thought I would have to find some little Eskimo village,

you know, some place with one of those wild, bushwhacking pilots who take off in blizzards—"

One eyebrow went up. "You won't find Resolute Bay exactly a metropolis."

"Does he actually take people to the Pole? I mean, land so you can walk around. Maybe plant a flag, like Peary?"

He propped his elbows on the counter and made a steeple with his fingers. "So we understand. We haven't received specific information on it, but we hear MacIntosh has flown a few tourists right to the Pole. Why don't you write to him, or telephone?"

"Beautiful," I said. I thanked him and turned to leave.

I had reached the door when I heard him clear his throat. "Uh, by the way—"

I turned back, waiting.

"Dress warmly."

Barnes laughed. I mean, really laughed out loud. This is an event that occurs only once or twice a year, so whatever he was thinking must have been pretty funny.

"Of course you can take a few days off to go to the North Pole. Five thousand dollars is quite a bonanza. I think you should have it."

My first reaction was pure joy. Then I had some nasty second thoughts. Obviously I wasn't very important to the operation if he was so quickly willing to dispense with my services during this crucial part of the investigation. What kind of a dope was he to let me go off this way?

"You sure you can spare me? I mean, the investigation is really at an important stage."

"Well—" Barnes thought about it. "I think it would be worth while for one of us to keep an eye on Kathryn. A trip to the North Pole with her might be very revealing."

Revealing what? The sound of her teeth chattering? "She's not going. She has a sinus condition which won't permit it."

Barnes understands sinus conditions. "Oh. That's too bad. However, she has to go."

"She does?"

He nodded. "I went over a copy of Kilgore's will with Shunk. I'm very familiar with all the provisions." He rubbed his chin, thinking. "She probably doesn't understand it, but she definitely has to attend the scattering."

I stood up and stretched. "She'll finagle herself out of that little chore. Probably already has a note from her doctor saying it may be harmful to her health."

He smiled. "As a lawyer, I can tell her she's receiving very poor advice, if that is what her lawyers have advised. She's got to go. The will plainly states, 'Should my wife Kathryn be unable, for reasons of health or otherwise, or unwilling, to attend the ceremony of scattering my ashes on the North Pole, my estate is to be apportioned as follows—' If she doesn't attend, four fifths of the estate go to the Osborne Kilgore Memorial Wing of Gotham Hospital."

"Oh."

"He even added instructions stating specifically that she must attend in person, and not by proxy, surrogate, deputy, or stand-in. If she wants to give Gotham Hospital twelve million dollars, she can skip the fun. Otherwise"—he shook his head—"no *way*."

I telephoned Kathryn.

"I've decided to accept the assignment," I said.

"I'm so glad. Did Mr. Barnes agree?" Her voice was as creamy as tapioca.

"Yes. Incidentally, he's a lawyer, you know. He says you'd better check with your lawyers. He has read the will, and he says that unless you attend the scattering in person, you will most certainly lose four fifths of the estate. There's no possible out for you, unless you want to give most of the estate to Gotham Hospital."

There was a long silence. "He's certain?"

"Absolutely."

"I can't believe it. What utter nonsense!"

"Barnes is a good lawyer. You'd better check on it."

"It's absolutely ridiculous! I'm not going to any goddamned North Pole!" The phone banged down at her end. I rubbed my right ear.

135

15

Sergeant Marino ran his palm over his bald spot wearily. "I wish I had something for you, Barnes. I've covered the whole damned fracas again and"—he shook his head—"nothing."

Barnes leaned back in his chair. "I appreciate your coming in this evening, when you're off duty."

Marino shrugged. "That's okay." He reached for a stack of papers near the corner of his desk. "These are all statements, depositions, and reports from my people. If you want to go through them, you're welcome."

Barnes accepted them, nodding.

"You see, our biggest problem, by the time we knew Kilgore's death was anything but a straight drowning, everything had been cleaned up. All the leftover food had been ground up in the disposal and flushed down the drain. All the plates, glasses, silverware, tables, anything else connected with the party, had been washed or cleaned thoroughly. There's just no physical evidence whatsoever."

Barnes leafed through the papers quickly, then put them down. "I think I'd like to talk to the two servants who were in the kitchen most of the day." He smiled apologetically. "Not that I expect to bring out anything new. Put it under the heading of leaving no stone unturned."

Marino rested his chin on his fist. "You could talk to Carola Bogen. Maggy O'Connor, the cook, is in Ireland."

"Ireland? Kathryn Kilgore didn't by any chance donate the trip?"

Marino lifted his chin, smiling. "You're as suspicious as a lousy cop, Barnes. No, her old mother is very sick. Strictly a family emergency."

Barnes thumped the papers idly. "I suppose I might as well talk to Carola Bogen. What sort of woman is she?"

"Girl, not woman. Real little sexpot. Plays dumb, but smart as hell underneath. Got more nerve than six Siamese cats."

"Oh." He turned and looked out Marino's one big window at the lighted State Police parking lot below. "In that case, Larry would probably get more out of her. She can *relate* to him." There was a touch of whimsy in his use of the word *relate*. He thinks we spend entirely too much time relating.

Marino straightened up. "I'll telephone and see whether she's at home. She only works at Swigatchit when the Kilgores are in residence."

Barnes turned to me, smiling. "I'll stay here and go over these statements." He handed me the keys to the Porsche. "Be careful driving my car, dammit. Go over what happened the day of the cookout in the minutest detail. Don't do anything you'll be ashamed of tomorrow."

Marino chuckled, picking up the phone. He telephoned and found that Miss Bogen was at home, and would be glad to see me. He replaced the handset and said to Barnes, "Why don't I have one of my people Xerox these for you? We can go out for a drink while it's being done."

Barnes stood up. "Good. That way you won't have to wait around while I read them."

The Bogens lived in a neatly painted little frame house just off Main Street in Swigatchit Village. There was a sign on the big bay window which read 'Antiques.'

Carola Bogen answered the door. "My mother's gone to the movies in Powell and won't be back for *hours*. Are you the man Sergeant Marino called about? I'm sure you are. Who else would be coming around in this dumb place?"

I guessed she was about twenty. She had long golden hair, magnificent legs revealed by a very short miniskirt, and nicely proportioned breasts partially visible above her low-cut, braless dress. Her face was okay too. She had big brown eyes, and long fake eyelashes.

"I appreciate your seeing me," I said.

"Come in. I like your mustache. How long did it take you to grow it?"

"About a month, I guess."

We went into the living room, which seemed to be pretty cluttered with antiques.

She sat down on one of the chewed-up old sofas. "Sit down. How old are you?"

"Twenty-five."

"I'm twenty-one." She slid one hand between her long hair and her neck and flipped it out, bouncing it a few times. Then she squirmed around on the sofa. "Are you married?"

"No."

"She gave her hair another flip. "How much do you make in your job?"

"Three hundred a week."

She moved closer to me. "How did you get the job? What do you do? Are you a New York detective?"

"No, I'm a private investigator. I got the job answering an ad in the paper."

She stood up. "I have a run in my panty hose." She bent over, lifting what little there was of her skirt, and examined the run carefully.

I stroked my mustache with one finger and tried to remain calm.

She sat down, this time very close. "Are you engaged?"

"Well, sort of."

Her long golden hair was hanging in my lap. "Would you like a drink? All we have is Scotch. My mother likes Scotch."

"Scotch would be fine."

"My mother is a widow. We live here alone." She squirmed herself to her feet. "My father divorced her."

I toyed with my mustache some more. "Sorry to hear that."

"Do you like Coke or ginger ale with your Scotch?"

"Just water, thanks."

She went out and came back quickly with a bottle of Clan MacGregor, one empty glass and a glass of water.

"Aren't you having any?"

"I don't drink. I don't even drink coffee." She poured a dollop of Scotch in the empty glass, then handed both glasses to me. Apparently the locals in Swigatchit drank their whiskey neat, with water for a chaser if needed. I added a little water to the Scotch, then put both glasses down. Her hair was in my lap again, her face very close to mine.

"If we were married, how much money would you give your wife every week?"

I took a gulp of Scotch, feeling her breath warm on my cheek. "I've never thought about it. Whatever she needed, I guess."

She batted her long eyelashes. "I can tell that you are a very *kind* person."

This wasn't exactly covering the day of the cookout in the minutest detail. I was tempted to forget all about the day of the cookout. On the other hand, Barnes wouldn't like it, and he had been very nice about letting me go to the North Pole. He would be expecting a tape. I was glad I hadn't turned it on yet. The guffaws would resound all the way to Wall Street.

I stood up and fumbled in my pocket, activating the recorder. Then I looked around, noticed an old wooden rocking chair, and pulled it over.

"I haven't sat in one of these in years."

She flipped her hair, smiling.

I decided boyish honesty was required. "Actually I moved over here because I'm having a tough time keeping my mind on what I came here for. To talk to you about Kilgore's death."

She grinned, flipping her hair more vigorously. "Okay," she said.

"You were in the kitchen all day? The day of the cookout?"

"In and out. Mostly in, I guess."

"Did you see Osborne Kilgore in the morning?"

"Sure."

"What was he doing?"

"When?"

"Each time you saw him."

She thought for a while. "The first time was very early. I took a pitcher of tomato juice cocktail mix to him in the breakfast room."

"This was all he had for breakfast?"

She squirmed a little, studying her beautiful legs. "He drank most of the tomato juice, but he didn't have breakfast until later. He went out and picked mushrooms, then he came back and had Maggy fix breakfast."

"The tomato juice cocktail mix was actually a pitcher of bloody marys, according to Mrs. Kilgore."

"You mean with vodka in it?"

I nodded.

"I didn't see anybody put vodka in it."

"Did he seem intoxicated to you when he left to pick mushrooms?"

She batted her eyelashes thoughtfully. "I didn't see him when he left. But I saw him when he came back, and he certainly didn't seem drunk."

"As I understand it, the mushrooms he picked were in a large wicker basket, and they remained on one of the kitchen tables until they were taken out to the cookout."

She nodded, pursing her lovely lips.

"Did you see anyone take any out, or put any in?"

"Uh-*uh*. We weren't supposed to even touch them. Once somebody washed them and there was an awful scene. It seems that if you wash them it wrecks their flavor or something."

"You mean, they cook them with dirt on them?"

She shook her head. "No, they're supposed to be wiped off with a damp cloth, or something."

"Who did this?"

"Maggy, with Mr. Kilgore watching."

"Were you there when Maggy prepared Mr. Kilgore's breakfast?"

She gave her hair another flip. "No, R.W.B. sent me on an errand to the caterers."

"R.W.B.?"

She smiled slyly. "Promise you won't tell her? Mrs. Kilgore?"

I nodded.

"We call her R.W.B. It means rich-witch-bitch." She giggled.

I continued my questioning for another half hour, but nothing significant came out. We'd have to check the statements of others who had been in contact with Kilgore in the morning. If he had not been drinking, as Kathryn claimed, it might give us a little something to go on.

As I made for the door she said, "What's your address in New York? I may come down to see you."

I grinned and said, "That'll be great. When are you coming? Thanks a lot for seeing me." I hurried out.

"What's your address?" she yelled after me.

I waved my hand and called, "Be looking forward to it. See you."

All I needed to make life pretty miserable was for Isabel to come upon Carola visiting me in New York.

16

Miller made it in to work dry-nosed and well, and this trip he could find no fault with our questions.

"You've got a nice set of graphs there. Too bad you can't take them into court," he said.

"I don't know," said Barnes. He tossed Kathryn Kilgore's graphs on the conference table and glanced at me. "These are certainly puzzling. They indicate that she knows definitely who killed Ossie, but that she's telling the truth when she says she didn't give him the poison mushrooms. On the other hand, the questions relating to whether she fed aconite to Eads indicate that she definitely killed him." He showed me the mountains rising where she answered these questions. "If she didn't murder Kilgore, what motive would she have for killing Eads?"

Miller rubbed his chin and looked blank.

Barnes turned to him. "Irwin, just how accurate would you say these things are? Not in indicating stress, but in indicating lying?"

Miller thought it over. "You established good conditions this time. The atmosphere was about as good as you could expect. The lies really stand out. In this instance I would estimate ninety-five to ninety-nine percent accuracy."

"Why not one hundred percent?"

He shrugged, smiling. "Because people are not computers. There are always unpredictable elements." He slapped the table gently. "Look at it this way. It's all a matter of evaluation. You kept the scene reasonably calm. If you find the subject is not showing stress in answering similar questions, why should she experience stress with this one? She must be lying. On the other hand, the human mind can go off on tangents. Suppose, for instance, that the question accidentally triggers some totally irrelevant but panic-producing thought? In fact, this can occur without even being triggered by the question. A man gets a sudden, pain in his chest from gas and thinks. 'My God, I'm having a heart attack!' This can happen once in a blue moon."

Barnes turned pale at the mention of a heart attack.

We dropped the subject and got to work studying Bentinck's graphs. According to the Dektor PSE, he was lying when he said that he didn't suspect anyone of putting harmful mushrooms in Kilgore's food, or of feeding aconite to Eads, but he was telling the truth when he said that he didn't do either himself, and that he didn't know definitely who did.

Christiana's graphs had exactly the same pattern. She suspected, but didn't know definitely, and didn't carry out either crime.

As we expected, Hal and Debbie Zimmerman were the same. They suspected, didn't know definitely, and didn't do.

We went back to Barnes's office to mull over this confusing picture.

According to the tapes, Bentinck, Christiana, Bold-Jepson, and Barbara Bold were innocent, and Kathryn Kilgore was guilty only of poisoning Eads. That wouldn't help Wicker-sham. Kathryn would have an adequate little defense budget of some twenty million dollars if she ever came to trial. Five million of it would be supplied sadly by Wickersham.

"Try this for size," I said. "Suppose Kilgore's death was genuinely an accident, and Kathryn killed Eads for some other reason?"

Barnes shook his head. "No, absolutely not. In that case there is no *reason* for her to kill Eads."

"No reason we know about."

He gritted his teeth. "We have researched these people and their relationships exhaustively. I do not, repeat do not, believe I have overlooked any reasonable possibilities."

When he gets nasty that way, there is no use arguing with him.

He said, "I for one will assume that the Dektor slipped up in the matter of Kathryn and the mushrooms."

"You could just as easily assume that it slipped up in the matter of Kathryn and the aconite."

He glanced at me pityingly. "Since it gave all the other major suspects a clean bill of health, what you are suggesting is that the Dektor analysis is completely useless to us."

I scratched my head. "I hadn't thought of that."

"You should try thinking occasionally. You'll find it refreshing."

I stretched out comfortably on the sofa. I think better relaxed. "That was unsporting and on the sarcastic side too," I said.

"That it was."

He pulled out his small notebook, made an entry in it, and reached for his cigarettes. "I'm going to assume that Kathryn is guilty of both murders." He lit his cigarette carefully. "There's only the small problem of finding some hard evidence to prove it."

"Nothing to it. We accuse her, and she confesses."

He smiled. "Yes, I can see it all clearly. We advise her of her rights, have her lawyers present, and they urge her to give us a full statement."

I sat up. "How about this? We trap her into a situation where she thinks she is going to kill us. In a burst of gloating, she brags about her crimes, describing them in complete detail. Then Assistant Deputy Inspector Superintendent Shunk steps out from behind a screen with eight witnesses and says, 'Madam, I must warn you—' "

He held up his hand. "Cease."

"Speaking of lawyers—"

The phone rang, interrupting me. Barnes picked it up.

"Yes, hello." He listened for a moment, then said, "I can't believe it. Ridiculous." He covered the mouthpiece with his hand and said to me, "They've arrested Christiana." Then he turned back to the phone. "When can I see Lieutenant Shunk?"

What motive would Christiana have? Her half of the five million dollars? It didn't seem too likely.

Barnes had hardly lowered the phone to its cradle when it rang again. He answered it, then motioned for me to take it.

It was Kathryn. "Larry?"

"Yes."

"This stupid North Pole business. Have you started to make any arrangements?"

"Well—I've found out how to get there. When it comes to actual arrangements, I'll have to have some money. First I have to fly to Montreal. Then I have to catch a Nordair flight to Resolute Bay. Then I have to charter a flight to the Pole. I don't know what that will cost. As near as I can figure it, getting to Resolute Bay and back will be about six hundred dollars."

There was a silence, then she said, "The lawyers say I have to go." Her voice sounded as though it was coming through clenched teeth.

"Oh. When do you want to leave?"

"I don't know, dammit. As soon as possible, I suppose." There was enough suppressed fury creeping through the wire to melt it.

"You want me to make all the arrangements?"

"No, I just called because your voice thrills me."

"As I said, I'll have to have some money."

"Come over and I'll give you a check." Bang. My right eardrum was again bruised.

I turned to Barnes, who had been listening with interest. "Madame Kilgore is North Poleward bound, due to some legal problems. She wants me to take her up there for the scattering as quickly as feasible."

"So I gathered."

"Shall I set it up to leave right away, or delay it for a day or so? I mean, this Christiana thing. Does it change the situation?"

Barnes rubbed his chin and thought about it. "My first guess would be, get on with it. However, let's go over and see Shunk."

Lieutenant Shunk was happy. He even shook hands with me.

"What have you got on Christiana Bold-Jepson?" asked Barnes, skipping the usual preliminary small talk.

"Open and shut," said Shunk. "She got herself bombed unconscious, with all the doors double-locked inside. Her husband got panicky and called us. Apparently she's been pretty depressed, and he was afraid—"

"I understand. We talked to her," said Barnes.

"One of my men went on the squeal. Being familiar with the case, he stayed behind and gave the apartment a quick shakedown. He had a right to, even without a warrant. Possible suicide attempt, dangerous drugs around, all that."

"And he found some aconite," said Barnes.

Shunk's bushy eyebrows went up. "How'd you know?"

"Guessed. I would also guess Kathryn planted it there."

Shunk waved his hand. "Oh, come on."

"No, I'm serious. Where was it found?"

"In the bathroom. In a small plastic pill container. Buried in a jar of cold cream."

Barnes nodded. "Easiest place in the world to plant it."

Shunk ran his hand through his taffy-colored crewcut. "But that's not all we found, buster. This aconite is crude, homemade stuff. It's made from the roots of the monkshood plant, and that's easy enough to find if you are a gardener."

"Kathryn is a botanist," interrupted Barnes.

"Wait a minute, buster, I haven't finished. This stuff was made by chopping the roots up and pulverizing them in a blender. There are traces of it in Mrs. Bold-Jepson's blender."

Barnes shook his head. "Now I believe it even less. She

146

may be cracking up, but she wouldn't leave the blender unwashed all this time."

Shunk threw up his hands. "Berk, you're being very contentious. You haven't even heard the whole story. The blender had been washed. There were minute bits of aconite which had worked their way into the housing of the axle that turns the blades."

Barnes stared at him silently for a few seconds.

Finally he said, "I suppose you've got a case. But I'm not at all convinced."

Shunk thumped the desk with his fingers. "Why are you so hipped on Kathryn Kilgore? It's true that she's a bigger beneficiary, but money in these cases is relative. There are guys who will kill for ten bucks. It's quite possible that the two million plus looks a lot bigger to her than five million looks to Kathryn."

Barnes told him about our Dektor graphs.

Shunk listened patiently, then shrugged. "Those graphs and thirty-five cents will get you a ride on the subway."

Barnes said, "I have confidence in them."

Shunk stood up. "These things can be helpful in an investigation, it's true. But when you have hard evidence—"

"Where is Chris? In the hospital?" asked Barnes.

"No, she just had an overload of booze. The hospital tidied her up and turned her over to us." He shuffled some papers, standing impatiently at his desk. "She's in a cell. The D.A.'s recommending no bail."

"What does she say?"

"Nothing. Won't utter a word." He glanced at his watch. "Look, Berk, I've got to cut this short. We can talk later, if you want."

Kathryn wasn't home, but Teresa, the maid, had an envelope for me. In it was a check for three thousand dollars, and a couple of lines scribbled on a piece of note paper which said, as near as I could figure out, "I want to take care of this tomorrow. Make all arrangements immediately." She thought we'd just pop up to the North Pole tomorrow, be back in time for an early dinner. I took the check to the savings bank where Isabel and I have our copout account. After considerable hassle I managed to cash it. Since it was a larger sum than the amount in the account, two vice-presidents had to come over and scrutinize my signature, making me do it over a couple of times just to be sure I wasn't cheating. They made me nervous, and both times the signature looked different from the one on their card. I told them I was going to have a word with Isabel about changing the account to the bank next door, where we could get a free rechargeable flashlight, or a bun warmer.

Back at the office I telephoned Resolute Bay and managed to get Sam MacIntosh's number without difficulty.

A young girl answered. "Is Mr. MacIntosh in?" I asked.

"No."

"Do you expect him back soon?"

"I don't know. Daddy's rescuing."

"Rescuing?"

"Daddy's rescuing two intrepid explorers who are stuck on an ice floe that's breaking up."

Ice floes breaking up? That sounded ominous.

"Would you have any idea how long it will take to rescue them?"

"No. Daddy has to fly around and see if there is any place he can land on the ice floe. But he can't fly around much because he has to have enough fuel to get back."

"If he can't land, what will he do?"

"He'll drop them some chocolate and stuff."

"Why don't they send for a helicopter?"

She giggled. "Mister, they're *way* out of copter range. They're almost out of Daddy's range."

"If we come up, will he fly us to the North Pole?"

There was another giggle. "Sure. If you've got the money, and he's got the time."

"How much?"

"Depends. You have to talk to Daddy about that."

"How cold is it up there?"

"In Resolute? It's warm today. Almost twenty degrees."

"Fahrenheit? You mean it's twelve degrees below freezing?"

"Yep."

"How cold is it at the Pole?"

"Depends. Maybe minus twenty, maybe minus fifty."

"You mean, fifty degrees below zero *Fahrenheit*?"

"Yep."

I thanked her and replaced the phone thoughtfully. I'm strictly a summer outdoor type myself. I don't even like to sit around the fire and drink hot buttered rum, much less go out in that cold snow. And when the icy winds blow, I turn blue. Still, five thousand dollars was a lot of bread. You really can't turn up your nose at that kind of bread. So I'll suffer a little.

Barnes came in and I showed him Kathryn's note.

"Shall I go ahead tomorrow, as ordered?"

He smiled. "Why not? Maybe under the strain and danger of the North Pole she'll break down and confess."

"You think it's dangerous?"

"Of course it's dangerous. Blizzards come on without warning, icy gales a hundred or two hundred miles an hour whip around the ice floes, the temperature can be eighty to a hundred degrees below freezing. Why, it's the most treacherous spot on the whole earth."

I swallowed hard. "Of course, the plane would be heated," I said. "They wouldn't fly around there without a heated plane."

He laughed. "Just kidding you. It's probably not too bad in late spring. Why, it's almost June."

"The pilot's daughter said it could be twenty to fifty degrees below zero at the Pole."

He looked at me. "Really? You'd better take warm clothes."

"It may take a few days. As far as I can figure out, the Pole is about a thousand miles from Resolute Bay. I have a feeling you don't just step in Mr. MacIntosh's plane and fly up there and back in a few hours. The weather's probably got to be just right."

Barnes nodded. "Few days or not, you might as well go. My last hope is Maggy O'Connor. I have been trying to get her to telephone me from Galway. There's no phone in her home. But she hasn't called. The poor soul may be frightened at the idea of making a trans-Atlantic call, or not understand about reversing the charges."

"Maggy O'Connor? Oh, you mean the Kilgore cook."

He nodded. "If I don't hear from her tomorrow, I'll take a run over to Ireland and talk to her."

I get the North Pole, he gets Ireland. But that was unfair carping. I was getting five thousand for the North Pole. Considering the dangers, maybe I should ask for ten?

There was no problem with reservations. I scheduled us for a 7 A.M. flight to Montreal, which arrived in plenty of time for connecting with the Nordair flight to Resolute Bay. Then I called Kathryn and told her to meet me at the Air Canada desk at Kennedy at six-thirty.

"My God! That early?"

"If we miss the eleven-fifteen flight from Montreal, there isn't another one until the next day."

"Damn. That's the middle of the night."

"You'd better dress very warmly. They tell me it can be twenty to fifty degrees below zero at the Pole."

"Oh God!"

"And Kathryn, don't forget to bring the ashes."

I got pistol-whipped in the ear again, and we were disconnected.

I went home and searched my wardrobe for warm clothes. The best I could come up with was two pairs of thermal underwear, a heavy Connemara sweater, a heavy tweed sports jacket, my winter overcoat, and a ski mask left over from my one experience with this thrilling sport.

Isabel wasn't too happy with the idea of my going to the North Pole with another woman, so I promised to take her on the next trip.

17

Kathryn arrived at the Air Canada desk wearing ski pants, a mink coat, and a heavy woolen scarf tied over her head. She was clutching a brass urn in one hand, which I presumed contained Kilgore's ashes, and a small overnight case in the other. The temperature was about sixty-five degrees.

"Aren't you hot in that outfit?"

"Hot? I'm not even awake. Get me coffee."

"Can't. Last call for boarding was five minutes ago."

She handed me the ashes. "Get me on the goddamned plane. Get me to the North Pole. Get me back to civilization. I'm so sick of this whole business I could frow up."

We hustled aboard.

Kathryn sulked all the way to Resolute Bay, which was okay with me since I didn't feel very talkative myself. I didn't know what to do with the ashes. I held the urn for a while, then decided that since the lid seemed to be tightly sealed, I could slip it under the seat. I slept all the way to Montreal. When we left the plane, I forgot the ashes and had to go back.

The stewardess was pretty suspicious, thinking maybe I was coming back to plant a bomb. She accompanied me to the seat and watched while I retrieved the urn.

"What is that?"

"It's Osborne Kilgore's ashes. The famous writer."

"Osborne Kilgore's ashes?"

I could tell she thought it was pretty stupid of me to forget them. "I'm not sure you should have carried ashes in the passenger compartment. A corpse has to go in the baggage compartment," she said.

I tucked the urn under my arm. "But ashes are small and neat, and not offensively packaged," I said.

Her eyes widened. "You know something? You give me the creeps."

Frankly, it gave me the creeps, carrying Kilgore's ashes around. Especially when we were having lunch on the flight to Resolute. I wondered if any of them might have gotten on my hands. I went to the lavatory and washed them thoroughly. After two martinis and a reasonably good lunch I went back to sleep, a somewhat troubled sleep in which Osborne Kilgore, pale and blue-lipped, accused me of sitting on his ashes, and not handling his final rites with proper respect and ceremony. When Kathryn woke me up I was explaining somewhat lamely that since I was neither undertaker nor minister, I did not dig this kind of deal at all.

"I hope you thought to make hotel reservations. We might not be able to fly to the Pole this afternoon." She was looking out the window. "There's absolutely nothing down there but"—she paused—"I don't know what's down there."

"Ice and snow and water? Kathryn, Resolute is a village of about two hundred people. There's no Northwest Territories Hilton. In fact, there isn't any hotel at all. We'll probably have to get rooms with some widow lady."

"Oh my God! Maybe we can go to the Pole right away?"

"I doubt it. It's already late in the afternoon."

The loudspeaker system went on. "Folks, there's a very bad crosswind at Resolute. There will be considerable turbulence as we descend and land. Tighten your seat belts and hang on."

The next ten minutes were among the most thrilling in my life. We bounced and plunged and leaped like an angry stallion, then hit the runway with a crash that I was sure would split the plane from end to end. Only after the reversed engines' roar slowed us down did I realize that we were still whole and rolling safely to a stop.

We stepped off the plane into nippy New York winter.

Kathryn shivered and pulled her mink coat tighter. "Where are the cabs?"

I didn't bother to answer that one. We carried our suitcases and Kilgore's ashes over to a small frame building which served as airport waiting room and office. Its sole occupant was a youngster reading a paperback.

"Where would I find Sam MacIntosh?" I asked.

He lowered the book and placed it carefully face down, then looked up. "His hangar is about a hundred yards down to the left. But you won't find him there. He's flying an Eskimo kid to the hospital."

"What happened to the two explorers he was rescuing yesterday?"

"They're still out there. Couldn't get down."

"That's terrible."

"Oh, they'll be okay. He dropped them a good supply of food."

Kathryn, who had been listening impatiently, asked, "Where can we get rooms?"

He turned to survey her somewhat mussed-up beauty. "Pretty hard to say, ma'am." He shook his head. "Town's pretty full up. Lots of rich nobs up here fishing and photographing this week. You might try Clarence Amarakiyak. He's got some trailers he rents."

We left our suitcases and Ossie with the boy and went in search of Clarence Amarakiyak. The road through the tiny village was free of snow, and the air seemed bracing and pure after Manhattan. I took a deep breath and became dizzy with so much oxygen. The village consisted mostly of small, one-story frame houses widely spaced. We passed one general store and a diner, and then came to Clarence Amarakiyak's trailer park.

He was a smiling little Eskimo, stocky and broad-shouldered.

"I got one trailer left. Beautiful trailer. Comfortable."

"We need two," said Kathryn.

He kept grinning. "Only one left. Last room in town."

We followed him to the beaten-up old trailer and climbed in to inspect it. Reasonably clean, it contained two bunk beds, one on each side, a kerosene space heater, a table, two straight chairs, and a small galley with a two-burner butane stove, water tank, and sink. There was even a small chemical toilet tucked in a corner and screened off with a shower curtain.

"We'll take it," I said.

He glanced at Kathryn's mink coat. "Thirty-fi dollahs a night."

The Hilton wouldn't have any trouble with their rates when they finally got there.

"Is there somewhere we can get a drink?" I asked.

"You like whiskey? I bring you a bottle. Ten dollah."

I gave him the ten dollars. Kathryn sank down on one of the bunks and said, "Jesus H. Christ."

I sat down on the other bunk and looked at her. "MacIntosh will probably be back tonight. Maybe he'll fly us up the first thing tomorrow."

She fumbled in her coat, brought out a cigarette and lit it. "Just don't get any funny ideas because we have to sleep in the same room."

"Don't worry. I know your heart belongs to the reverend."

She smiled, smoke curling around her lips. "That's a rather quaint way of putting it."

As a matter of fact, she had absolutely nothing to worry about. Barnes believed that she had poisoned two men, and Barnes was usually right. This sort of dampened her sex appeal. To me, she was about as tantalizing as one of Susan's hairy tarantulas.

"I'll go get the bags," I said.

Amarakiyak returned with a fifth of Black and White Scotch and a squarish package wrapped in wax paper. At least we were getting a reasonable return, by Arctic Circle standards, for the ten dollars.

"What's that?" Kathryn asked, looking at the package.

Amarakiyak grinned. "You hear of beluga caviar?"

"Of course."

"This beluga blubber. Great delicacy. Called muktuk. Come all the way from Siberia."

"Ugh."

"You try it, you like it. Eskimos call it breakfast of champions."

He opened a cabinet above the butane stove and brought out three glasses, placed them on the table, and poured us each a generous shot.

"We drink to your safe arrival. How come you're here? You take pictures? You no fish, hunt, that for sure as St. Joseph."

"We want to fly to the North Pole. We understand Mr. MacIntosh will take us."

He gonked down his Scotch in one swallow and nodded. "He take you if he not too busy." He poured himself another generous jolt. "I got a friend in Seal Cove. He fly there all the time. Nice ship. Twin-engine prop jet, two-thousand-mile range. Bob Mulligan. Great pilot." He tossed down his second drink, wiped his mouth with the back of his hand, and began to untie the package of beluga blubber.

"Would he take us to the Pole if MacIntosh can't?" asked Kathryn.

He tore off a piece of the blubber and handed it to Kathryn. Kathryn handed it right back. He offered it to me. I shook my head. "Not right now. I'm not hungry." I poured myself another drink. Kathryn hadn't touched hers.

"Go good with whiskey," said Amarakiyak.

"Thanks anyway. I'll save it for later."

He turned to Kathryn. "Bob Mulligan fly you if MacIntosh too busy."

He stood up. "You got baggage at the airport? I'll fetch it back here."

I finished my drink quickly. "I'll go with you. I want to check on MacIntosh again."

We climbed into Amarakiyak's battered old pickup truck and traveled the half mile or so back to the airport in about thirty seconds of riding interspersed with thirty seconds of bouncing.

I handed him the two suitcases and the urn. "Be careful with the brass vase," I said. "It's a valuable heirloom." I had read somewhere that Eskimos are very superstitious about death and anything belonging to a dead person. There was no use finding out how he would react to Ossie's ashes.

He stored the urn and the suitcases carefully in the back of the truck, then followed me as I strolled down to the MacIntosh hangar. It was well labeled with a sign saying MACINTOSH AVIATION.

The only occupant was a freckled-faced little girl of twelve or thirteen.

"I think we talked on the phone yesterday when I called from New York," I said.

She smiled. "You're the man who wants to go to the North Pole."

"That's right. When do you expect Daddy back?"

"Who knows?"

"I mean—"

"He flew the little boy to Yellowknife. Maybe he'll be back tomorrow morning. Who knows?"

I scribbled a note to MacIntosh, telling him where we were staying, and asking him to let us know about the trip to the Pole.

I thanked her and turned back to Amarakiyak who had caught up with me and was standing there with his perpetual grin. "Guess we might as well go back to the trailer," I said.

"Okay-dokay."

We got in his truck and bounced our way back to the trailer camp.

"You have vase?" asked Amarakiyak, clutching the suitcases.

156

"No. It must still be in the truck."

We looked. The truck bed was starkly empty.

"Maybe it bounced out," I said.

Amarakiyak shook his head. "Never. Some bastard stole."

"I think it bounced out. Who would want to steal it?"

"You say valuable heirloom. Some bastard stole."

I put the suitcases in the trailer, nodding to Kathryn, and went back to the truck. "Amarakiyak, we've got to find that vase. Let's drive back to the airport slowly. You look on one side of the road and I'll look on the other. It must have bounced out."

His grin faded for the first time. "No find that way. Some bastard stole."

I climbed in the truck. "If somebody stole, he stole bad luck. That vase contains a dead man's ashes."

"Dead man's *what*?"

"Ashes. The lady I am with was his wife. He died. It was his wish to be cremated, and to have his ashes scattered over the North Pole. That's why we're here."

He stared at me, mouth open. "Oh boy."

"So you see, we've got to get those ashes back. I don't dare tell the widow."

"Oh boy."

He climbed in the driver's side and we started our slow trip back to the airport. We made the trip twice, getting plenty of eye strain, but no urn.

Amarakiyak turned to me. "My friend, you do have a problem. Indeed, a grievous problem." The accents were English major, U.S.A.

I stared at him, startled. "What happened to the friendly nigger routine?"

He laughed. "Rich white man likes to be cheated by simple savage. Proves that all men are as inherently dishonest as he is. Can't stand being bilked by uppity Princeton graduate. Brown man doesn't know his place when he becomes Princeton graduate."

I nodded, still a little dazed. "I see your point."

"I think I know what happened to your friend's ashes. We have some pretty ratty kids on this island, both Eskimo and white. And I know who most of the little bastards are."

"Oh."

"On top of that, I saw four of them around the airport while we were there. Good place to start, right?" He slapped my knee. "Don't worry, my friend, I'll get your ashes back. You go console your widow. Some chick, eh?" He poked me gently in the ribs. "You got it made, man. I could see you drooling when you found there was only one trailer left."

Drooling was in the eye of the beholder. Amarakiyak was the one who was drooling.

"Thanks. I sure hope you can find it," I said. "Want me to come with you?"

He shook his head. "Nope. The little ding-dongs will tell me the truth. They know Uncle Clarence. With you there, they'll freeze."

I went in and told Kathryn the bad news.

She did some nasty screaming, commenting fulsomely on my stupidity in between yelps. After she ran out of breath she lay on her stomach and pounded the pillow with both fists.

Finally she calmed down and I persuaded her to drink the Scotch Amarakiyak had poured for her earlier.

"Stop worrying. Clarence knows the kids who stole it. He'll get it back."

"Suppose they emptied it?"

I hadn't thought of that. Finding nothing but ashes they might well have dumped the works to use the urn for some other purpose. A place to store whale teeth, or maybe a choice hunk of beluga blubber. I poured us another drink.

"As my grandpop used to say, quit crossing your damned bridges until you get to them."

"Oh, shut up."

"How about a nice blubber steak at the diner? It may taste better hot."

Silence.

"They might even have a regular steak."

"I'm not hungry."

"Then I guess I'll go eat alone."

"Go ahead."

"Can I bring you back a ham sandwich?"

"No."

"Cheese sandwich?"

"No!"

I strolled down the road to the diner and had a big bowl of thick vegetable soup, a sirloin steak with french fries, apple pie à la mode, and coffee. If there were any rich nob fishermen, hunters, or photographers around, I didn't see them. The only other customers in the diner were two Eskimos and two weatherbeaten, bewhiskered locals. Neither, I was certain, had ever chaired a board of directors' meeting.

When I left the diner I noticed that it was getting to be more like a Chicago winter than a New York winter. A bitterly cold gale was howling across the wide-open spaces, and the ground was crunchy underfoot with crackling new ice.

In the trailer, Kathryn, apparently asleep, was just a mound under three heavy blankets. It was eight-thirty. I couldn't remember ever having gone to bed at eight-thirty. On the other hand, the facilities for entertainment seemed pretty limited. I'd forgotten to bring anything to read, and the light wasn't very good in the trailer anyway. That left walking back up to the diner for another piece of apple pie à la mode, and it hardly seemed worth plowing through the gale.

The temperature had dropped sharply in the trailer. While icicles weren't exactly forming at the end of my nose, I felt they would be shortly. I tried to light the space heater, but somehow couldn't find the right combination. I turned some knobs and held a match in several different places and achieved nothing but a stronger smell of kerosene. I put on my overcoat and went out to look for Clarence Amarakiyak, but there was no light and no answer in the trailer marked MANAGER.

I was going to bed at eight-thirty whether I liked it or not.

159

I stripped down to my thermal underwear and crawled under the heavy blankets. Since I had slept most of the day, sleep was not likely, but at least I was warm.

I was lying there with my eyes closed when Kathryn said, "Larry, are you awake?"

"Yep."

"I can't sleep."

"Neither can I. Maybe a drink would help." I raised myself on one elbow, pulled the chain of the table lamp, and looked at her. All I could see was a nose and one eye.

"It's awfully cold in here. Why don't you light that stove?"

"I tried. Do you know how to light it?"

She poked her head further out of the blankets. "Me? I never saw one before in my life."

I reached for the bottle and poured us each a stiff drink. We sat up with our respective blankets pulled up under our chins. I leaned across the aisle and handed her the drink.

"Talk to me. Tell me your life story," she said.

Anything to pass the time.

"Yours would probably be more interesting."

She sipped her drink. "I doubt it. My father taught botany and never made more than fourteen thousand dollars a year in his life. And since my mother was in the hospital all the time, we were usually about fourteen thousand dollars a year in debt. I never had anything except what I stole."

"Stole?"

"I used to shoplift most of my clothes and cosmetics. Sometimes I could steal some very nice things when I was baby sitting."

She sat up higher in her bed. "If you ever say I told you this, I'll say you're a liar, and I'll sue you for slander."

"Kathryn, I wouldn't dream of violating your confidence on something like this."

"I'm not sorry I did. Children shouldn't be brought up without anything."

I was astonished. "Didn't you ever get caught?"

"Twice. I cried and said I was sorry and they let me go."

I shifted my weight and took some more Scotch. Straight, it burned, but I was too lazy to get up and put water in it.

"I never did anything illegal but smoke pot."

"Pot's nothing. Everybody smokes pot." There was a silence as she stared at me, her lips curled in a faint smile. "Do you have a girl friend?"

"Yep."

"Are you sleeping with her?"

"As frequently as she'll let me."

Kathryn giggled softly. "What's she like?"

"She's beautiful. Bright too."

"Are you going to get married?"

"Someday, probably."

"What's holding you back?"

I thought about it. It was not easy to explain. Kathryn wasn't much more than five years older than I was, but somehow she seemed a part of a different generation. Maybe it was because she had been married to the famous Osborne Kilgore.

"I don't know. I guess we haven't quite got it all sorted out, as our British clients would put it."

"Do you love her?"

Love was one of those things people had so many different ways of defining. "I suppose so."

"Aren't you sure?"

"Depends on how you define it."

"What?"

"Love."

"Oh." She put her now-empty glass on the table and slid back down under the covers. "Men are all alike. Bastards."

"What did I say wrong?"

"Nothing. I'm going to sleep."

I reached for the chain of the old-fashioned lamp and pulled it. I had begun to feel a little drowsy and warm from the Scotch.

I'm not sure how long I had slept when I woke up

161

shivering. The wind, which had been muted before, was now howling, and the trailer trembled and rocked when some of the hard gusts hit it.

I turned on the light. Kathryn was awake, her teeth chattering.

"I'm freezing to death," she said.

"We're way up in the Arctic Circle," I said, my own teeth chattering. "You've got to expect it to be a little chilly."

Kathryn sat up, stared around wildly, then worked herself out of the tangle of blankets and stood up. She was still wearing her ski pants and sweater.

She quickly gathered up her blankets and dumped them on my bunk.

"Move over. This isn't an invitation. It's survival."

It wasn't a very wide bunk. I moved over as much as I could and she slipped in beside me, shaking and shuddering. She pulled herself very close, her breath warm on my chest, and lay there alternately trembling and sighing.

With six blankets and the warmth of our bodies, the chill gradually disappeared. Kathryn turned over and squirmed a bit until her back was plastered tightly into the bend of my body. Her neck was resting on my right arm and it soon became a little cramped. In moving it, my hand inadvertently settled on her breast. Perhaps it was vertently, because had she been Isabel, that's about where my hand would have been.

She reached up and squeezed my hand gently, then pushed it away. "Don't, please," she whispered.

"Sorry." The whole thing was ridiculous. With her plump rear end pressing tightly against a very sensitive portion of my anatomy, she was concerned about my hand touching her breast. I turned over and faced the wall. She squirmed close again, clutching me.

Anyway, my back wouldn't get cold, that was for sure.

The whole idea of being excited by this sexy, bad-tempered, arrogant, possibly murderous woman irritated me. The fact that we were plastered together in a narrow bed

162

to alleviate the arctic cold was only a practical necessity. But face it. Cold or no cold, she had crawled into my bed and was clinging to me tightly, arousing me with her female equipment of breasts and thighs and rounded buttocks and long black hair. If I made love to her, I would feel pretty cheap later in helping Barnes send her to prison. I was glad there was no electric chair waiting. I had a momentary vision of Kathryn strapped in this monstrous instrument, bolts of artificial lightning sizzling through her body, making it jerk against the straps, releasing her bowels and bladder to foul the air around her. I was no longer aroused.

But I still couldn't fall asleep. Kathryn, however, had done so, and I could feel her shallow, regular breathing mildly tickling the back of my neck. I began to doze.

"What?" I asked, waking up.

"The wins slur Bob," she muttered, and I realized that she was talking in her sleep. She made a few more unintelligible sounds, then sighed deeply. Then she said something that sounded like "Mores on my hands. Wash."

I was getting tired of lying on my left side. I said softly, "One, two, three, *turn*," and turned over, not thinking it would work. It did, however, and she turned with me.

Sleep came eventually. But not for long. I was awakened by Kathryn sobbing gently.

"What's the matter?"

She sniffed. "Bob should be here with me. I begged him to come. It's the one time in my life I need him desperately."

The Reverend Bob had real problems at home. "I can see where he wouldn't be able to leave Chris when she's in such serious trouble."

"Chris!" It was more of a venomous hiss than a word.

"How can you expect—"

"I *need* him." Her voice trembled. "I've done everything for him. Chris is nothing. *Nothing.*"

"She's his wife."

"Oh, shut up," she sobbed.

We both drifted back into fitful sleep.

There was a banging on the door and it popped open. Clarence Amarakiyak climbed in bouncily. "Ah, a good, good morning to you, my friends." He was holding the urn up for us to see. "I found your parcel. There are two lads with very sore bottoms this morning." He placed it carefully on the table next to the bottle of Scotch, then looked at me slyly, since Kathryn and I were still huddled together in my bunk.

"Thank God," murmured Kathryn, sitting up.

"How do you light that damned stove?" I asked. "We practically froze to death because I couldn't get it lighted."

"We were sleeping together to keep warm. Not what you think," said Kathryn.

Amarakiyak's face fell. "Oh, too bad," he said. I had a feeling he was sad because we said we didn't make love. He bounced up the aisle and lit the heater quickly. I got up and watched him closely, feeling self-conscious in my long thermal underwear.

"You get breakfast in the commissary if you hurry. Better than diner."

"Commissary?"

"Department of Transport Commissary. Very good. Very clean."

"I'm hungry," said Kathryn.

"You should be. You didn't eat any dinner."

"MacIntosh is back. But he can't take you to the Pole today. He has to fly more supplies to those fellows stuck on the ice floe," said Amarakiyak.

Kathryn got out of bed and stretched. The trailer was warming up. "Can Mulligan fly us?"

Amarakiyak fondled our bottle of Scotch, which was now about half full. "I telephoned him last night. He'll try if you want."

"Try?" I asked.

"Weather's chancy. He'll fly you to the Eureka weather station, where he's got to stop to refuel anyway. That's about two hundred miles from the Pole. Then if the weather is holding, he'll fly you on to the Pole. Otherwise you have to come back here and try again."

"Jeeze." It had sounded so simple back in New York. Kathryn was washing her face at the sink. "Wow, this water is cold!"

"Make your cheeks rosy," said Amarakiyak.

Outside in the sun it was almost warm, though I estimated that the temperature was about twenty still. Clarence drove us to the commissary in his old truck. It was another low, sprawling frame building, and we were able to stoke up on sizable helpings of Canadian bacon, toast, scrambled eggs and coffee. As we were leaving I saw MacIntosh's daughter and paused at the table where she sat eating a big bowl of hot porridge.

"Daddy's flying back to the intrepid explorers, I hear."

"Yes. No North Pole for you today."

"We may fly up with Mulligan."

"Mulligan!" Her turned up little nose tilted higher. The competition wasn't even worth discussing.

I remembered that Barnes had instructed me to report daily on Kathryn and the status of our trip to the Pole. Kathryn had gone on ahead with Amarakiyak, offering an opportunity for me to stop at the telegraph counter and send a quick wire. What could I say about Kathryn? That I had slept with her, but that I hadn't really compromised our position by fraternizing with the enemy? What was there to report? I scribbled hastily, "In sleep talk subject said quote mores on my hands period wash period unquote hope to fly to Pole today regards Larry."

We went back to the trailer where Amarakiyak outfitted us for the polar flight. He brought over heavy wolfskin parkas, and two pairs of Eskimo boots made of reindeer hide, and four dogskin mittens.

"I don't need all this crap," said Kathryn. "We're just going to fly over the Pole, dump the goddamned ashes, and fly back."

"Suppose you come down in a snowstorm, or you get weathered in at Eureka?" asked Amarakiyak. After all, he was getting fifty dollars' rent for the equipment. On the other hand, it might be pretty darned cold. Howling winds. Ice barriers. Snowstorms. Maybe minus twenty to minus fifty temperature. While he was putting the stuff in the truck I hurried back into the trailer, undressed, and pulled on my second set of thermal underwear.

I checked the back of the truck to be sure that the urn was tucked well under the arctic clothing so that it couldn't bounce out. There was a large cardboard box I hadn't noticed before.

"What's this, Clarence?"

"Food. Never travel arctic without plenty food," he said, lapsing into his friendly native role.

It sounded ominous. I could picture us stranded in a blizzard, nibbling a can of cold potted ham. Still, the round trip would take seven or eight hours, I estimated, even if things went well. We had to fly nine hundred miles to the Pole and nine hundred back in a ship that cruised at about three hundred miles an hour, plus a stop at Eureka for refueling. The food would come in handy.

Seal Cove is a small mining settlement about thirty miles northwest of Resolute. Someone, Amarakiyak explained, had discovered a small vein of gold there two years ago, but nothing had developed since and interest in the place was petering out. The airstrip was nothing but hard-packed snow and ice. At Resolute one runway was kept clear for the 727 to land on wheels.

Bob Mulligan was waiting for us in his rickety, patched-up looking hangar. He was a tall Irishman with red, curly hair, and a wild look in his cold blue eyes. According to Amarakiyak, he had been an R.A.F. pilot but had defected to the I.R.A. during the troubles in Belfast. Later, for reasons unknown to Amarakiyak, he had defected from the I.R.A. Being in trouble on both fronts, this remote arctic outpost seemed like a good idea.

Smiling, he shook hands with us. "Clarence says you want to drop some poor soul's remains on the North Pole."

"My husband," Kathryn said tightly. "We don't *want* to, but he requested it."

"It's not the first time I've flown such a mission. Poor old soul wanted to be buried in the Aran Islands, and we flew her over by helicopter. Dropped her twice, poor old soul. Luckily the coffin floated."

Kathryn turned her head, annoyed.

"My fee will be fifteen hundred dollars if we make it. Seven hundred and fifty if we have to turn back."

I wasn't in a mood to quibble. Chartering a plane for a flight to the North Pole wouldn't be cheap.

"With seven hundred and fifty in advance," he added.

I counted out the seven hundred and fifty and handed it to him. The exchequer was getting low. I had just about enough left to pay the remaining seven-fifty. I hoped Kathryn had brought her checkbook.

The aircraft, I was glad to see, was a modern Fansa two-engined prop jet, and relatively new. I helped Amarakiyak load the food, our arctic clothing, and the urn into the cargo space behind the seats. Kathryn and I climbed in and waited.

Mulligan turned his head. "Fasten your seat belts, folks. It may be a little bumpy on take-off." He didn't mention anything about extinguishing cigarettes; in fact, he had a lighted one hanging from his lips.

We roared across the ice and were quickly airborne. I borrowed one of Kathryn's cigarettes. I successfully gave up smoking in college, but the occasion somehow demanded it. I was on the way to the North Pole, an adventure not many people would have, following in the footsteps of Peary, Cook, Wally Herbert, and other great explorers.

"You've flown over the Pole many times, I expect," I said to Mulligan.

"Several, not many."

"Have you ever landed there?"

"Once."

"It must have been a thrill. To stand on the spot where Peary planted all the flags and all that."

Mulligan turned back to look at me. "Frankly, I don't think Peary really made it. This is the opinion of a number of arctic experts."

I was familiar with the controversy. "Possible," I said. The cigarette tasted wonderful. I'd have to be careful or I'd be back on them.

Kathryn was asleep. This girl could sleep anywhere, and did. Even locked in my dispassionate embrace.

I looked out the window. The sun was a great hazy ball near the horizon. Below there was nothing but ice and strips and triangular patches of black water. Occasional lines of barrier ice jutted up twenty or thirty feet where ice floes had come together with a crunch. It went on and on, unchanging, mile after mile.

Mulligan twisted slightly and handed me a pair of binoculars. "Look ahead, about two o'clock. You'll see a polar bear."

I focused the glasses, staring at the ice. It was a polar bear all right. He was lumbering along like a fat old man on his way to the supermarket. Through the glasses the water looked blue-black instead of black.

"He's looking for his dinner."

"What?"

"Seal. They search for air holes where the seals come up."

I nudged Kathryn. "Kathryn, there's a polar bear down there."

She opened her eyes. "What did you expect, tropical fish?"

"Don't you want to look?"

"No." She closed her eyes. "I've seen a polar bear."

Gradually the sky became overcast and dark, and the ice below was indistinct in the gray haze. A slight chill ran up my spine. What could be more desolate than the polar icecap? Compared to this the Sahara would be literally teeming with life. We had traveled for hundreds of miles and seen nothing but one lonely old polar bear.

I settled back and tried to doze, but my senses were too alert. Below there was now nothing but dirty white mist.

"Will you have enough ceiling to land at Eureka?" I asked.

He shrugged. "It was three hundred feet there five minutes ago."

"That's pretty low."

He talked briefly into his chest microphone, then lit a cigarette casually. "If we can't get down, we'll just have to head back to Seal Cove."

I was almost ready to head back to Seal Cove anyway. There was something eerie and frightening about flying through this thick, white mist at the top of the world. At least, there were no high mountains to crash into. We'd have to be pretty low to hit an ice barrier.

We rumbled on through the mist for another hour.

"We're going to descend," said Mulligan. "We're on instruments, but we should break through at about two hundred feet."

I held my breath. For a few seconds, anyway. We broke through the fog, but Mulligan had overshot the runway. The motors roared as he accelerated to gain altitude.

"Give it another try," he said, banking sharply to the left.

We descended again, this time breaking through in perfect alignment. We hit the snow so smoothly that I didn't realize we were on the ground until he reversed the engines.

Through the mist the Eureka weather station was just some yellow lights. "Do we get out here?" I asked.

"It'll take ten or fifteen minutes to refuel. If you want to stretch your legs, go ahead. Not much to see."

Kathryn said, "I'll stay in the plane."

He nodded. "Just don't smoke while they're pumping fuel."

"I think I'll stroll a bit," I said.

I stepped out of the plane into a gentle breeze that froze both ears solid. I pulled my overcoat collar up, wondering whether I should climb back into the plane for the wolfskin parka.

Mulligan thumped me on the shoulder hurrying past. "Nippy, eh? I'm going in and speak to one of the weather officers."

The fuel truck was a snowmobile. Two parka-clad men hopped off and began cheerily to fill the tanks.

I was stamping my feet, trying to keep warm. "Hot coffee over in the tent," said one of them.

The fog was clearing a little and I could see that there were several pyramidal tents near the airstrip, and the usual low frame building in the background. I said, "Thanks," and stomped my way over to the nearest tent.

Mulligan was there, chatting with a short, stocky man also clad in a parka. He introduced him as Sergeant Hansen. There was a big coffee urn, cups and a plate of donuts.

"Have some coffee," said Hansen. "It's thick as mud and black as the devil's heart."

I thanked him and filled one of the cups. It was everything he said it was and more. I added more milk and sugar.

"I think we're going to be okay for the Pole," said Mulligan to me. "It's clearing."

"That's great," I said, munching a donut.

I stomped back to the plane and asked Kathryn if she wanted coffee. She didn't.

Mulligan came along in a minute, paid his gas bill, then climbed into the cockpit whistling "We're Off to See the Wizard."

Kathryn murmured something that sounded like "Good God."

"What's the matter?"

"I hate this cold, stupid wasteland. It's—it's desolate. I want to get back to New York."

Mulligan turned. "It's not desolate at all when you get to know it. Awesome, perhaps. But great beauty and grandeur. And strength." He rolled the words out sonorously.

"I don't want to get to know it."

"Your privilege, madam." He gunned the motors and we crunched out to the runway, paused briefly, then roared off into the mud-colored haze.

I looked out the window. More ice, ice barriers, snow, and black paths of water.

"It's a little monotonous. Like driving hour after hour through the wheat fields of Kansas," I said.

Mulligan lit a cigarette. "I grew up in the middle of a few square miles of wheat fields in Canada. By comparison, the arctic is jumping with action, believe me. The entire surface here is nothing but ice floes. They're always moving, breaking apart, crashing together."

He handed me the glasses again. "Look down about three o'clock. You'll see a barrier being formed."

I focused on a fairly wide strip of dark water which was rapidly becoming narrower. Then the two ice floes came together with a thunderous crash we could hear even above the roar of the engines. A high ridge of ice shot upward, forming a miniature mountain range that seemed to extend for miles.

Mulligan stared down at the newly formed barrier. "That's why it takes so long to go anywhere up here by land. You have to hack your way through or over those damned things."

"How long until we'll be over the Pole?"

He checked his charts and instruments. "About twenty minutes."

The clouds had almost all cleared away, but the sun was still only a red hazy ball close to the horizon.

"Beautiful," said Mulligan. "We couldn't ask for better weather."

Kathryn stirred sleepily. "Let's dump the ashes and go back. This is close enough."

With the brighter sky, the ice began to look cleaner, the water bluer. I reminded myself that we were looking at the deep, cold Arctic Ocean, covered only with a thin, rubbery, gray-white skin. "We're almost there. Better dot all the *i*'s. You know how lawyers are."

I looked over Mulligan's shoulder at the array of complicated controls and instruments. According to the compass we were flying almost due east. This puzzled me until I remembered that the magnetic pole is about on the same latitude as Resolute, but west of Resolute.

"Eighty-nine degrees fifty-nine north," said Mulligan. "We are about a mile from the Pole and will be over it in approximately twelve seconds. I'll start descent and circle."

I reached for the urn, unlatched the top, and held it in readiness while counting the seconds. "—ten thousand, eleven thousand, twelve thousand," then stared hard. Below was the famous North Pole. The imaginary dot in the very center of the top of the world that had fascinated so many generations of explorers. As we descended, I could see that the surface was smooth and white with a light snow cover.

"Perfect," said Mulligan. "Couldn't ask for a better landing strip."

"I don't want to go down. Dump the ashes," said Kathryn.

In seconds we were down and skimming along over the powdery snow.

"I asked you *not* to land," said Kathryn.

Mulligan reversed the engines, slowing the ship to a crisp halt. "As captain of the aircraft, I make all the decisions about landing or not landing." He twisted around to look at her. "You should be pleased, madam, that I'm providing you the opportunity for a dignified committal of your husband's remains." He looked at me. 'Dump the ashes,' she says. Are we carrying garbage? An ashtray to be emptied?"

Kathryn muttered, "Oh, shut up."

"Are you daft, woman? Have you no respect for the dead?"

There was an uncomfortable silence.

"Come on, Kathryn," I said cheerily, "you'll probably be the first woman in history to actually stand on the North Pole."

She glared at me. "I didn't come here to make records. I came here to comply with a thoroughly vicious provision in a will."

We struggled into the wolfskin parkas, pulled on the boots and mittens, and eased ourselves through an aircraft door that had become suddenly smaller.

I was standing on the North Pole. Me, Lawrence Howe. Top that one if you can.

I had been wondering what to do about the ceremony. You don't just dump the ashtray. Osborne Kilgore had been a human being. These were his last rites. But I had no idea what to say. I turned to Mulligan.

"As captain of the aircraft, isn't it your duty to conduct the committal rites?"

Mulligan shivered, stamping his feet. He was wearing a parka, but it was a light, canvas-covered garment. "I'm not a churchgoing man. I was raised in the mass, but I haven't been in a church since I was ten years old."

"Neither have I."

He shuddered. "Give me the urn. What was the poor chap's name?"

"Osborne Kilgore."

He stood with his legs apart, his eyes raised heavenward. "O Lord, we commit the remains of this poor sinner Osborne Kilgore to your tender mercy. Accept this poor sinner who has violated thy laws by having his mortal body reduced by fire to ashes; forgive him his transgressions, we ask this in the name of the Holy Christ." He paused. "And you'll be forgiving this poor sinner for not remembering the Latin."

He nudged me. "Stand aside, man, you're downwind."

I moved out of the way. He turned the urn over and shook it. The gray-black ashes were caught in the wind and peppered the snow for some distance. He placed the urn upright on the snow, then turned to me. "Enjoy the North Pole for a few minutes if you wish. I'm going to get back in the aircraft." Kathryn was already climbing in.

I walked a few yards upwind, not wishing to tramp on Osborne Kilgore's ashes. Here I was standing on the North Pole, and there was no camera to record the momentous occasion. We'd get signed statements from Mulligan, of course, and each sign as a witness. For the lawyers. Who was going to believe I had stood on the North Pole? I took a deep breath of the icy air, then headed back to the plane. Even with the wolfskin parka, the chill was settling in, and the wind was turning my nose into a blue icicle.

I climbed in the plane, slammed the door, wriggled out of the arctic outer clothes and stowed them behind the seat.

Mulligan had produced a fifth of Johnnie Walker Red and three plastic cups. "Now we'll be drinking a toast to Osborne

Kilgore, may his soul rest in peace. I somehow feel we slighted the ceremony."

"I don't want anything to drink. I want to go back," said Kathryn.

I accepted the cup, raised it, and said, "Well, good luck, Osborne Kilgore, wherever you are."

Mulligan lifted his. "Aye. Good luck, Osborne Kilgore. May your stay in purgatory be short." He zonked down his drink in one long, soft gurgle. Then he reached for the bottle and poured himself another cupful.

"Hey," I said, "as pilot, should you, uh, be drinking that much?"

He lit a cigarette, smiling. "Ah, lad, if you don't drink a jar or two in this climate your bone marrow freezes solid. Crack your block if you're not careful."

A groan which could have emanated from a chorus of a hundred men filled the plane.

"Uh-oh," said Mulligan.

"What is it?" I yelled.

A series of ear-splitting reports reverberated. Sound waves shook the cabin, bringing with them a noise like a multitude of forty-five-caliber pistols being fired in close quarters.

Kathryn put her hands over her ears and screamed.

"What is it?" I yelled again.

"A lead is forming."

"What the hell is a lead?"

"An ice floe is breaking apart."

"*An* ice floe?"

"Our ice floe."

We huddled, shoulders hunched, while the noise continued. Finally it tapered off, and the plane quit shuddering.

Mulligan tossed down the rest of his drink, then struggled into his parka. "Well, lads and lassies, it's time to reconnoiter. I hope there's enough of this ice cake left to get us airborne."

I pulled on my reindeer boots and wolfskin parka and followed him out the door. Kathryn sat huddled in her seat, her face expressionless.

I hurried along behind Mulligan, occasionally slipping in

the snow, as we headed down what was left of our runway. The water was farther away than I thought, and I felt somewhat relieved. It lapped against the ice, black and cold, because the sky had darkened to deep twilight. I was beginning to feel numb all over. The wind velocity had stepped up, cutting through my parka and both sets of thermal underwear.

"Is there enough left for a take-off?" I asked. We couldn't go in the other direction, that was certain. The surface was as rough as a boulder-strewn quarry.

Mulligan stared down at the widening black path. "A little chancy, but I think so."

I turned back in the direction of the plane. "Then let's get the hell out before something else happens," I said, my teeth beginning to chatter.

Snow started falling, at first gently, in big soft flakes. Soon it was a blinding torrent of gray-white, cutting visibility to a few feet. It took us fifteen minutes to locate the plane.

We stumbled in, two thirds frozen and hardly able to climb the three steps up to the cabin.

"You stupid son of a bitch, I told you not to land. Now you'll get us all killed," said Kathryn, with a sort of toneless venom.

Mulligan reached for the bottle. "Shut up. Speak when you're spoken to, woman." He filled two cups and handed me one. I drank about half of it immediately, the liquor burning my throat going down but spreading warmth through my body.

"So what do we do now?" I asked.

He shrugged. "Wait out the blizzard. I need every yard of that runway for take-off. If I can't see where it ends, we'll go in the drink. Very bad for the aircraft."

"How long might it last?"

He lifted his cup. "Who knows? Several hours, several days."

I glanced at my watch. Only 2 P.M. It already seemed like several days, and we had been gone from Seal Cove less than five hours.

"I suppose we ought to break out some food." I crawled back into the cargo compartment and opened the box Amarakiyak had provided. Standing in one corner was another fifth of Black and White. Thoughtful of him. Spam, Underwood deviled ham, sardines, crackers, canned beef stew, corned beef hash, baked beans, and other assorted cans were packed neatly. There was even a loaf of bread.

I pulled out one of the cans and the loaf of bread. "Anybody want a Spam sandwich?"

There was no answer from up front. I had a feeling Mulligan was going to drink his lunch, and we'd have a gone pilot on our hands, even if the snow stopped. Kathryn would continue to sulk, probably.

I cut a thick slice of Spam with the knife Clarence had included, made a sandwich, and carried it back to my seat to eat. Kathryn was staring straight ahead, ignoring me. Mulligan was drinking.

I was hungry, and the rough sandwich tasted good. I munched away, thinking this might be my last meal on earth. All we needed was for the ice floe to rip across closer to the aircraft or—who knows?—right beneath it. We would settle into those black, frigid waters like a dying seagull.

Mulligan was having a muted conversation with his microphone. Maybe all was not lost. MacIntosh might drop us supplies. We might even be rescued by snowmobile from the Eureka weather station.

"You lousy, stinking, miserable, vicious bastard," Kathryn muttered.

"Who, me?"

"Ossie. He meant for me to die."

"Don't be asinine, woman," said Mulligan, upending his cup.

I handed him my cup. The bottle was getting pretty low. "Give me another drink before you run out of booze."

He filled my cup, a dead butt hanging from one lip. "Don't worry, chum, there's plenty more where that came from."

I was afraid of that, and had deliberately not mentioned

the bottle in the case Amarakiyak had packed. "Are you going to be sober enough to fly this thing if and when the snow stops?" I was getting pretty irritated.

"Ah, well, that's the question. To live or die, get drunk or stay sober." He lit a fresh cigarette shakily. "If I had a sweet colleen to keep house for me, it might make a difference. Of course, they'll catch up with me, sooner or later."

"They?"

"My chums from the old sod."

"They're coming all the way up to the arctic to get you? Just for coping out?"

He took another swallow. "Well, there's a little more to the story than that. To take a hypothetical case, suppose a man was entrusted with a half million dollars to buy arms for his chums? Suppose the man had already decided the whole bloody conflict was a pile of worthless excrement, and that both sides were bloody well crazy? Suppose this man bought himself a beautiful aircraft with the money?"

"I see." It was a better use for the money, all right.

The temperature in the cabin was about forty, but perspiration popped out on my forehead. It was too much. In addition to cracking ice floes, weather foul-up, and a bitchy widow, I had to contend with a drunkenly depressed pilot on the lam from the Provisional wing of the I.R.A. I took a big jolt of whiskey and then borrowed one of his cigarettes and lit it.

"They'll never find you, Mulligan. If they come up here, you can fly to some remote little Mexican village."

He perked up. "Ah, well, that's true. I could have a lovely little Mexican colleen to keep me snug. With my beautiful aircraft, I can always be a thousand miles away from them. Like that." He snapped his fingers.

As we were talking, the cabin gradually became brighter. I glanced out the window. The sun was out! Still a hazy red ball near the horizon, but definitely shining.

"The snow's stopped! Let's go!" I yelled.

Mulligan smiled. "Now have you just noticed that?"

"Let's go. Quickly," said Kathryn.

Mulligan put on his parka. "Better take another look at our airstrip. We may have to clear some snow away from the runners."

Luckily the snow had changed from the wet flakes at the start of the snowfall to the dry, powdery stuff we were walking through. About four inches had accumulated, and was not enough, Mulligan estimated, to require unpacking the shovels he carried. We walked the length of the runway to where it ended at the water. The gap was about ten feet wide.

Mulligan looked back at the aircraft, studying the distance.

"Even if it's too short, wouldn't momentum carry us across the water to the rest of the runway?"

Mulligan nodded. "That it might. But you'll notice the other floe has tilted a bit. Its shore is a good foot higher."

"Wouldn't you have enough lift to get over that?"

He sighed deeply. "Ah, well, we'll see, won't we?"

We hurried back to the plane and climbed in. Mulligan started the engines, warmed them for a minute, then said, "Buckle in tightly. We've a devil of a crosswind."

He maneuvered the ship around slowly until we were headed in the right direction, then turned to us. "Pray if you feel so inclined." He crossed himself, gunned the engines, and we were skimming madly toward that black river.

I held my breath, watching it rush toward us like a film running wild. I almost yelled, "Stop! We'll never make it!"

The engines roared with every ounce of power he could give them. Then it was all over so quickly I found myself still holding my breath, waiting. We were bucking and tossing, but we were airborne.

It was the easiest five thousand dollars I ever made.

18

Barnes, Shunk, and Marino were waiting for us when we arrived at Kennedy.

I was glad to see New York. We had been weathered in for three days at Resolute Bay, and it had been pretty boring. We even tried muktuk, and found that it went well with Scotch, as Amarakiyak had predicted. I was mildly hung over. There hadn't been much to do but drink and eat and listen to Kathryn's bad-tempered nagging. I had begun to feel personally responsible for the bad weather.

Barnes shook hands with me and cuffed me warmly on the shoulder. "It's good to see you. You did a great job."

I thought he meant getting to the North Pole and coming back alive. "I stood right on the damned Pole. I've got an affidavit from the pilot to prove it." I was going to have it framed.

Barnes grinned. "That's great."

Lieutenant Shunk stepped up to Kathryn. "We'll have to ask you to accompany us to headquarters for questioning, Mrs. Kilgore."

Kathryn stared at him, her lips slightly parted. "I will not. I'm exhausted from this stupid trip. I'm going home and rest."

Shunk reached inside his jacket pocket. "In that case I will have to present you with this warrant I have for your arrest." He then read her the speech about her rights.

Kathryn listened, glaring at Shunk, Marino, and Barnes equally. "I'll sue you for false arrest," she said.

"That you can do," he said. He took her arm and they headed for the squad car parked outside the glass doors. Giving us a brief wave of his hand, Marino followed them.

"What's going on?" I asked Barnes. "When I left, Christiana was in jail."

"It's a hell of a mess," said Barnes. "Your telegram put me on the right track." We walked out to the parking lot to find his Porsche. "Maggy O'Connor helped," he said over his shoulder.

"You flew to Ireland?"

"Hmmmm."

"That 'mores on my hands' helped?"

"Indeed it did."

I climbed in beside him. "I can't figure it out. I put it in the telegram almost as a gag, because I had nothing to report."

He paid the toll taker and zoomed out of the lot. "It's tricky, but somehow 'mores on my hands. Wash,' reminded me of the famous Lady Macbee. But obviously Kathryn couldn't have blood on her hands, except symbolically."

We careened around a truck, then zipped back into the high speed lane. "Kathryn impressed me as being too cold-blooded to have any trauma about symbolical blood on her hands. The 'mores' were something specific, something physical, something relating to Amanita phalloides or aconite."

I grabbed the door. We were coming up too fast behind another truck, and the other lane was jam-packed with speeding cars. Barnes braked hard, tires screaming. We survived, the Porsche's hood coming up briefly under the rear of the trailer.

"That was close," I said.

"Hmmm."

We drove along in silence. I wanted to hear the rest of it, but the way Barnes drove, he needed to give it every bit of attention he had.

When we paused for a stop light he said, "With this in mind, I went back to the books on mushrooms and did some more studying. A link to the 'mores on my hands' phrase suddenly popped up. She had *spores* on her hands. Poisonous Amanita spores are a microscopic white powder. Harmless mushroom spores are beige-colored. As a botanist, she'd know the difference. She had 'blood' on her hands, physically."

I made appropriate noises of astonishment. I couldn't think of anything to say. We shot across the intersection and were away and weaving through traffic like a dog chasing a berserk cat.

"So she washed her hands," I said, when we stopped for another light.

"Right. But if she had Amanita phalloides spores on her hands, there was a possibility that she got them on something else. Such as the clothing she was wearing."

I breathed a sigh of relief when we pulled into the garage where Barnes parks the Porsche. Still, I might trip and break my neck stepping into the elevator in the Pan Am Building. This was my week for big risks.

"Since she's incarcerated, I take it that you found something incriminating?"

"We had good luck there. Maggy O'Connor was a big help."

"Oh?"

"She remembered exactly what Kathryn was wearing that morning. It was a chilly spring morning. Kathryn had gone for a walk early, before Kilgore came down. She had slipped on a white cotton raincoat. We found Amanita phalloides dust in the right pocket."

We left the elevator and started down the corridor to our offices. "That was a break," I said.

Our offices looked pretty good after Resolute Bay's rugged accommodations. Isabel would look even better.

"I want you to hear Maggy O'Connor's tape," said Barnes. "We still have some problems."

He switched on his large playback machine, spun the tape

past the opening chit-chat, and settled back in his swivel chair to listen. I perched on the arm of the sofa, half leaning and half sitting.

Barnes: Was Mr. Kilgore drunk when he left to pick mushrooms?

Maggy: Himself? Sober as a rent collector he was.

Barnes: Mrs. Kilgore states that he was drunk, that he consumed a pitcher of bloody marys. She further states that he slapped her when she remonstrated with him.

Maggy: The truth is not in her. The mister never drank until lunchtime. Nor did he ever slap her in my presence.

Barnes: Can you be certain of this?

Maggy: There was nothing in the tomato juice Carola took him. No liquor is kept in the breakfast room. As for the slap, the missus wasn't even present. He left through the kitchen door, and he was perfectly sober.

Barnes: When he returned, you prepared breakfast for him?

Maggy: Yes.

Barnes: Was Mrs. Kilgore present?

Maggy: Yes. Of that I'm sure. When I made the mister's mushroom omelette, she handed me two fat ones from the basket. "I'll need one more," I said. "He likes plenty of mushrooms in his omelette." "I'll get you another plump one," says herself, all smiles. Now I ask you, if the mister had slapped her, would she have been so helpful?

Barnes switched off the playback and sat there grinning. I slid down and sat on the sofa. "So the Dektor analysis was right! She was telling the truth when she said she didn't put any Amanita in Ossie's mushroom dish."

Barnes nodded. "We didn't ask the right questions."

There were a few more bits of circumstantial evidence to nail Kathryn. Susan Eads, who had been talking to Deborah, suddenly remembered that it was fresh horseradish Kathryn had offered Eads. He loved horseradish. Ground-up monkshood roots taste similar to horseradish. Mixed in with the real thing, the poison would have been unnoticeable. Shunk also had a deposition from Teresa stating that Kathryn had borrowed Chris's blender. The Kilgore blender was broken.

Both Shunk and Marino had good cases, but the evidence in the Kilgore murder was much stronger, and Kathryn would be tried first in Pell County.

The whole thing seemed to be nicely tidied up. "So what problems do we have?" I asked. I felt a little let down in playing such a minor role in the wrap-up. "Wickersham's probably off the hook for five of the ten million. They should be very happy. So what's more to do?"

"They're ecstatic. We're in line for a big bonus."

I liked that "we."

"There are complications. Shortly after you left for Canada, Bentinck Bold appeared at Shunk's office and confessed all. It was an obvious move to save Chris."

He consulted his little notebook and then lit a cigarette. "After testing him on a few items, Shunk refused to accept his confession. Bold couldn't pick an Amanita phalloides from a group of harmless mushrooms, even though they left on the famous 'collar,' which is a dead giveaway." He smiled at the unplanned pun. "He couldn't pick out a monkshood plant from a half dozen others of very different structure. He obviously didn't know the form in which the aconite had been administered, claiming that he obtained it from some medicine and dropped it in Eads's drink."

"Gallant of him."

"I believe there is more involved. I sat in on the questioning. There was something more on his mind than saving his sister."

He took Maggy O'Connor's tape from the machine and fitted another in, then turned it on.

Barnes: Did you do away with Osborne Kilgore?

Bentinck: Yes.

Barnes: By administering inedible mushrooms?

Bentinck: Yes.

Barnes: In previous interviews, did you tell the truth about your conversation with Osborne Kilgore the night he died?

Bentinck: Yes.

Barnes: Do you know why he changed his clothes late that night?

Bentinck: No.

Barnes switched off the player. He searched through some papers on his desk and found the right envelope. "Now take a look at these Dektor graphs," he said, handing me the strips. I studied them. It was amazing. According to the Dektor, Bentinck told the truth when he said that he "did away" with Osborne Kilgore, lied when he said he did it by administering inedible mushrooms. He was also lying when he answered the last two questions "yes." He hadn't told the truth about his conversation with Kilgore, and he *did* know why Kilgore changed his clothes.

"Fantastic," I said.

Barnes crushed out his cigarette carefully. "It is, indeed. I wonder just what the hell happened that evening. There's one more peculiar fact. I had the clothes left on the beach analyzed by Shunk's laboratory. They were not worn by Kilgore that evening."

"Not worn?"

"They had been freshly laundered. Even if he had worn them for as much as one or two minutes, minute traces of body oils and perspiration would be present."

"Very peculiar."

"It is. I think we'll have to have another session with Bentinck."

I had been hoping to have a shower, clean clothes, and dinner with Isabel. But as Grandpop used to say, "Get your goddamned business out of the way before you take your pleasure."

Bentinck wasn't at Bold House. He was in Washington, but expected back early in the evening. I was off duty until 9 P.M., since Barnes did not want to interrupt their dinner.

Having just returned from the Arctic Circle, I should have been immune to the chill which permeated Isabel's apartment. I had showered, shaved, and put on my best suit, and I pressed the buzzer carrying a box filled with a dozen roses.

She threw the box on the floor and stamped on it.

It seems that some skunk in Shunk's office leaked an item to *The News*. The case had been solved by Lawrence Howe, Barnes's assistant, who had obtained his lead through a remark the suspect had made in her sleep. "Howe, still up in the Arctic Circle with the suspect, was unavailable for comment," said the story, which she shoved under my nose.

"I can explain everything," I said, and did.

She listened, but I'm not sure she believed.

I rescued the roses from the battered box, put them in a vase, and added water.

"You never brought me flowers before," she said. That proved I was guilty right there.

"Dammit," I yelled, "I just felt like bringing you flowers. I almost got killed up there at the North Pole. The last thing I thought about before I almost died was you."

"I still don't see why you had to sleep with her."

"Look, if you were as cold as we were, you would have slept with Count Dracula."

19

Bentinck Bold answered the door himself. "Ah, the man with the check. I hope," he said. Then, seeing the look on Barnes's face, added, "No, I can see you don't have the check. You'd better come back to my study."

We followed him down the hall to the pleasant room at the back of the house. He stood by the door while we entered, then closed it carefully.

"Have a seat," he said, then strolled over to the swivel chair behind his big desk and eased himself into it.

"We'll try to make this brief," said Barnes.

Bentinck gestured with his hand. "No hurry. I'm feeling quite relaxed this evening. Chris is back at work, and all is well with Bold House."

"I take it she has resolved her problems with her husband?" said Barnes.

Bentinck nodded. "I hope so. When he saw how much trouble she was in, I think it shook him. Anyway, he rushed in to stand by her with every resource—"

"As you did," said Barnes.

Bentinck blushed faintly. "I'm afraid I acted a bit simpleminded."

"Not at all," said Barnes. "You had a powerful sense of guilt pushing you."

The atmosphere frosted slightly. "Just what do you mean by that?"

Barnes brought out the Dektor graphs and explained them

to Bentinck. Standing by the desk, and using the blunt end of his thin gold pencil as a pointer, he indicated the ups and downs of Bentinck's lies and the one true statement he had made: the "yes" to the question, "Did you do away with Osborne Kilgore?"

Bentinck leaned back in his chair and said, "What kind of bloody nonsense is this? You can't tell me this material would be admissible in court?"

Barnes went back to his chair. "Let's agree that it is going to be extremely difficult to prove. On the other hand, we have certain things going for us."

"Such as what?"

"Such as a theoretical reconstruction of the situation which could implicate you strongly. For instance, the Dektor says you lied about the conversation you had with Kilgore the evening of his death. It says you lied about his changing clothes. Why?"

Barnes toyed with his package of cigarettes, then took one out and placed it in his mouth, leaving it unlighted. "One could reconstruct the situation this way. You found Kilgore mortally sick by the pool. He probably understood that he had been poisoned by Amanita phalloides. People who know as much about wild mushrooms as he did would recognize the symptoms. He asked you to get a doctor."

Barnes paused to light his cigarette, staring at Bentinck over the lighted match. "If you called a doctor, he might survive. It was a great opportunity to get five million dollars with little risk. You picked him up and carried him down to the beach, staggered out into the water, and dumped him there. In the morning, Chris found his body and came to you. When you saw him, you suddenly realized that since he was clothed, suspicions would be aroused and an investigation would follow."

"Good God," said Bentinck.

Barnes continued in a calm voice. "You quickly stripped him, disposed of his salt-water-soaked clothes. Then you obtained a towel, fresh clothes, moccasins, and placed them on the beach."

Bentinck shook his head wonderingly. "Barnes, you have a

filthy mind. A man would have to be a psychotic monster to carry out such a brutal, cold-blooded act." He turned to me. "Larry, do I look like a psychotic monster to you?"

I smiled. "No, but I have great confidence in the Dektor analysis. It's been right almost every step of the way."

Barnes said quickly, "Perhaps there was a stronger reason. Let's say Kilgore knew he had been poisoned by wild mushrooms. He would undoubtedly know that your sister is also an aficionado. She was the only other wild-mushroom hunter in the group. You would also know this. Let's say Kilgore accused your sister of poisoning him. You realized that he would continue these accusations, if able, after the doctor arrived. For all you knew, it was possible that your sister *had* done it. You thought so the other day, and made a false confession to save her."

Bentinck continued to shake his head.

"It's too bad. Kathryn may even get away with it," said Barnes, puffing his undocumented cigarette gratefully.

"Why?" asked Bentinck.

"Because you both participated in killing Kilgore, but he actually died from drowning. He might have survived the mushrooms with prompt medical treatment. If I were her lawyer, I would make a big issue of the clothes, of your movements that night. I would investigate you until I turned up every possible answer."

Bentinck said, "Oh, for Christ's sake."

Barnes held up his hand. "One very weak spot is Chris. I'm sure, for instance, that when she first saw the body it was clothed. Possibly she heard you two quarreling the evening before. I have a feeling that something more than her husband's infidelity put her into a tailspin."

Bentinck lit a cigarette and inhaled thoughtfully.

"Suppose," he said finally, "that the participation was much more innocent than you visualized. Suppose the two men were walking on the beach and they became involved in a violent argument. Suppose Kilgore made some very insulting and very false accusations, and that the other man hauled off and popped him one on the button. Suppose,

188

realizing that the other participant was mad enough to beat the cupcakes out of him, Kilgore ran into the water and swam away?"

Barnes leaned over and crushed out his cigarette, jerking his hand back as a coal burned his thumb. He smiled. "That version makes more sense, I'll admit."

I said, "If the police bought it, the worst charge they could bring would be concealing evidence."

"Unfortunately, Kathryn's lawyers won't buy it. They'll harp on the proposition that your fight with Kilgore actually caused his death. They may even try to convince the jury that Kathryn picked the Amanita phalloides by mistake," said Barnes. "The more confusion, the better chance of creating a reasonable doubt."

Bentinck got up and started pacing back and forth near the windows. "There's quite a gap between the mere evidence of the clothes on the beach and my having a fight with Ossie. I posed this only as a hypothetical alternative to the ridiculous accusations you were making." He turned on his heel and stared at Barnes. "But if you accept it, why are you so anxious to crucify me?"

Barnes shook his head. "I'm not."

"Well then?"

"Wickersham has ten million dollars at stake in this situation. They could conceivably argue that both you and Kathryn were equally guilty in causing Kilgore's death. *They* may not accept your version."

Bentinck nodded, the trace of a small cynical smile breaking through. "And you'd help them. To cut off the five million for Bold House."

Barnes was silent for a moment, two fingers pressing his forehead above the left eye. I reached for the Bufferin.

"It's a difficult question. I owe them a full report on my investigation. If they choose to interpret it differently than I do . . ."

I've never seen Barnes look so genuinely uncomfortable.

"I believe your story," he said after another long pause. "But I have no right to set myself up as judge and jury. It seems to me that the only honest thing I can do is give Wickersham what I believe are the facts. I will, of course, include my opinion that your version is the truth."

Bentinck's eyebrows went up. "And what would this mean? That is, what do you think it will mean?"

Barnes shrugged. "Unfortunately our adversary system almost guarantees the answer. The whole thrust is always to win the case, not to see that justice is done. Wickersham's lawyers will be under strong pressure to save the company five million dollars. This offers a powerful incentive for believing that you share guilt with Kathryn."

Bentinck nodded. "Yes, of course." He thought for a moment, lighting another cigarette.

"What if I withdraw my claim?"

I handed Barnes a couple of Bufferin, which he accepted with a hurt smile. "I would say they might have a strong incentive to accept my opinion of your innocence." He chewed up the Bufferin gloomily. "Bringing you in might just help acquit Kathryn, and would serve no purpose. There would be no claim to fight."

Bentinck sat down, sprawling back in his big, heavily upholstered swivel chair. "Let me think about it."

We went away and let him think about it.

Isabel and I decided to give Kathryn's check for five thousand dollars to the New York Public Library. Somehow it didn't seem right to keep it. Barnes thought this was noble of us. In fact, he was so impressed he is going to replace it with five thousand from the bonus Wickersham has promised him.

Bentinck Bold took off. He may be hunting polar bears in the arctic, or fishing in Brazil. No one knows where he is, and as far as I know, the police aren't looking. He told Chris he was tired of the whole damned hassle, and that he was going away to write a book. Bold House is percolating along nicely under her direction. Also, we understand Barbara Bold is packing for a trip.

We were sitting in the office talking about a new case when Barnes ran across the small copy of the Karsh photo of Osborne Kilgore. He tore it into several pieces. "I think sending this back to Kathryn would be useless."

I had forgotten all about it. "I wondered at the time. Why did you borrow it?"

He smiled. "You know that ultra-modern gadget you looked into at Bold-Jepson's church? The instrument that revealed that you liked girls, because your pupils got bigger?"

I nodded. "They had some pretty sexy nudes."

"That technique is literally thousands of years old. Chinese jade dealers were artists in its use. Chinese faces may be inscrutable, but their pupils are not."

He scooped up the photo scraps and dropped them in his wastebasket. "I thought it might be an interesting first step to see who really liked Osborne Kilgore."

"Who did?"

"Only Susan Eads." It was sort of pathetic, when you thought about it.